"Who are you? Why am I here?"

"I'm Dr. Silverman, a neurosurgeon at the Cleveland Clinic. You were hit by a car. You've been in a coma for three days. Now, can you raise your left hand?"

Val complied, lifting her hand two feet off the bed. "Ow! Everything hurts! I'm not dead, am I?"

"You're very much alive, Mrs. Bennigan, much to your family's relief." Dr. Silverman picked up Val's wrist to take her pulse.

"Mrs. Bennigan?" Val said slowly. Her voice, although quiet, held an ominous quality. "Who's *she?*"

"Why *you* are. You're Mrs. Bennigan."

"I am not!"

Joel listened in mounting horror as Dr. Silverman probed for answers to telling questions. Where she was born. Her current address. The president of the United States. . . .

It was unreal. Val was caught in some kind of time warp, putting her back two years ago, before she had moved to Kent. *Snap out of it, Val. Come back to the present, my love.*

"And who is your husband?" Dr. Silverman was asking.

Val looked indignant. "Is this some kind of joke? I'm not married!"

With a thud, Joel's back hit the wall, his palms flat against the cool surface. "Val, sweetheart, what are you saying?"

She regarded him quizzically. "Why are you calling me sweetheart? I've never seen you before in my life!"

UNA MCMANUS was born in Dublin, Ireland, and came to the United States nearly twenty years ago. Una makes her home in Columbia, Maryland, with her Pennsylvania Dutch husband and their three strapping sons. She enjoys telling earthly stories about divine love because the greatest Teacher of all was a storyteller. She formerly wrote for **Heartsong Presents** as Elizabeth Murphy.

Books by Una McManus (Elizabeth Murphy)

HEARTSONG PRESENTS
HP125—Love's Tender Gift
HP138—Abiding Love
HP154—Tender Mercy
HP185—Abide With Me

Tender Remembrance

Una McManus

Heartsong Presents

A note from the Author:
I love to hear from my readers! You may write to me at the following address: **Una McManus**
Author Relations
P.O. Box 719
Uhrichsville, OH 44683

ISBN 1-57748-269-7

TENDER REMEMBRANCE

Cover illustration by Jeanne Brandt.

PRINTED IN THE U.S.A.

one

Should she admit he was right?

Or should she just bite her tongue and swallow it into the bargain?

Frowning, Val glared out the window next to her desk in the church office. That her husband was right was as obvious as Eskimos in Alaska or shamrocks in Ireland. Again! She hated it when Joel was so disgustingly, inescapably right. Clouds, dark and heavy, crowded the mottled sky, harbingers of yet another winter storm. After two winters in Ohio, Val didn't think she could stand another temper tantrum from grumpy Old Man Winter.

Of course, it wouldn't do any good to throw a tantrum herself, although that's exactly what she felt like doing at the moment.

"Honey, I don't want you to go," said Joel Bennigan, leaving his sermon blinking on the computer screen. He crossed the assistant pastor's office, stopped behind Val's chair, and began rubbing her shoulders. "Weather's gonna turn nasty before long, and the roads will be treacherous. This storm will be worse than usual—an Alberta Clipper. Just look at that snow!"

Since Faith Bible Church was built on a hill overlooking the city of Kent, Val had a panoramic view. The sleepy college town—population about 30,000, including students—shivered under a white blanket of steadily falling snow. Snow, snow, and more snow. Even at two

5

o'clock on Saturday afternoon, most of the cars were already using their low-beam headlights.

Irritated, Val tapped her felt-tipped pen against her papers. These long, vicious Ohio winters, how she hated them! Coming from the milder Maryland climate, she couldn't seem to adjust to snow and freezing weather from December to April. Her feet didn't warm up until summer!

She sighed heavily and looked up at Joel. Tall and broad-shouldered in the cable-knit cranberry sweater she'd given him for Christmas, he was still the handsomest man she'd ever known. With his thick, tawny hair and his almost palpable strength and goodness, he sometimes reminded her of a warrior archangel in a child's picture book. As associate pastor for Faith Bible, Joel manifested God's ways by his own manly, gentle, faithful living of the gospel. But, handsome or not, at times Val found him maddeningly protective. Even after ten months of marriage, she was still getting used to his constant watching out for her.

"Joel, the TV weathermen predict only *light* flurries," she protested with a slight shoulder shrug. "Just flurries, not storms."

"Since when are weathermen reliable prophets? In ancient Israel, they used to stone folks who made false predictions, you know." Joel kneaded her shoulders steadily. She'd been hunched over her speech all morning, revising and updating. She wanted it to be perfect. Now, he could feel the tension knotting her muscles.

"Oh, Joel, I can't back out, you know that. Not at this late date! It's a county-wide youth retreat. Six churches involved. Tons of publicity, even radio spots. There'll be hundreds of kids. I can't let them down. Anyway, if you were giving the talk, I'll bet you wouldn't leave them in the lurch, Reverend Do-Your-Duty!"

Joel ground his teeth and kneaded harder. "I know, I know."

Sensing his hesitancy and eager to take advantage of it, Val hurried on. "Anyway, these teens need to learn about religious cults. That suicide group in the news— these UFO cults, cults on the Internet, teen Satanism, New Age cults infiltrating Christian churches. . .well, you know how strongly I feel about education being the key to keeping kids out of cults."

Val knew how easily a person could be lured into a destructive cult. When she'd begun her master's degree in journalism at Kent State University two years ago, she herself had infiltrated a local cult for her Investigative Journalism class project. Since she knew about the indoctrination techniques of food and sleep deprivation, coupled with manipulation of fear and guilt, she'd figured she would be immune to the cult's influence. Joel had warned her to stay away from them, but she hadn't listened.

How wrong she'd been! Once she'd been isolated at the cult's rural brainwashing camp, Val had found herself succumbing just like the new recruits. Fortunately for her, Joel had eventually succeeded in rescuing her, risking his life in the process. That was a little over a year ago, shortly before they married.

But many young people remained trapped in cults, and more were being recruited every day. Since her own escape, Val had lectured about cults to youth groups, college students, mothers' clubs, to any audience that would listen. She'd even gone on Christian radio and authored several magazine pieces. As an ex-cult member and now as a pastor's wife, she took seriously her obligation to expose these wolves in sheep's clothing.

She'd never canceled a talk before, and she was loathe to consider backing out now. She had given her word. But, even so, she was secretly dreading the drive to Cleveland. In fine weather, the trip took forty-five minutes. But today, in this slushy, sleety mess, she'd be on the road at least an hour and a half—or more if there'd been an accident—before she reached the downtown church hosting the youth rally.

There was nothing she'd rather do than spend the afternoon in the warmth of her husband's office, catching up on her course work, joking with Joel, a pot of cappuccino and maybe a few fudge brownies from Brady's Coffee Shop. Just being around Joel was enough to make her happy. Snatches of conversation peppering their work, their little jokes, their habit of interrupting each other. Yes, she loved this man and she loved being with him.

Nothing doing, Val! Not today. You've got promises to keep, and miles to go before you sleep! Quit being such a wimp!

She sighed, wrestling with herself.

Gently, Joel pressed the pads of his thumbs into the kinks in her neck, talking as he worked the ache out of her muscles. She found his voice—so mellifluous and powerful from the pulpit—as soothing as his hands. His absolute earnestness made him a good preacher, and he was earnest now. Oh boy, was he earnest about keeping her home!

"I know education is the antidote to cult involvement, honey, babe, love of my life," he almost crooned. "I love you for caring so much about kids, but I don't want anything to happen to you. Nothing against your driving, but you're just not used to Ohio roads in a storm."

Val found herself bristling. She tried not to take offense where she knew none was intended, but she was irked. "Don't forget that defensive driving course you pressured me into, Joel Bennigan. And, in case you haven't noticed, I've already survived *two* winters here—and, guess what? I'm still alive! I can hold my own on bad roads. You native Ohioans aren't the only winter drivers in the country, you know!"

Joel stopped massaging and leaned down, nuzzling her ear. She swallowed hard as he moved closer, then she exhaled deeply and felt her tension untangling. The warmth of his breath sent shivers coursing through her. "My love, my life, my heart," he whispered, "what would I do if something happened to you?"

She tilted her head toward his, locking his eyes. Her heart leapt at the sight of his face. How had she ever lived without this man? Joel had pulled her out of the wintry loneliness that had been her life—the only child of an alcoholic mother; father, killed in Vietnam. As the result of her mother's disease, Val had known little love or caring. All she'd known of love was abandonment and soul-destroying bitterness.

Until Joel Bennigan. In the last two years, he had become the source of light in her dark life. His love had helped her believe more strongly in God's love.

Now Joel was running his hands through her long mass of chestnut curls, and Val found herself powerless to resist. She closed her eyes and sank into his embrace. He trailed kisses along the nape of her neck and let his lips rest in the warm hollow between her neck and her shoulder.

Even with closed eyes, Val could see Joel's Nordic

blue eyes, his light brown hair, his powerful physique that betrayed his former life as a college football star. She could see the way his broad face lit up when she walked into a room, as if he were starved for the sight of her. Who would have thought she'd find a love like his this side of heaven? There wasn't a day that Val didn't give thanks for God's tender gift of Joel Bennigan.

" 'I am my beloved's and my beloved is mine,' " murmured Joel, quoting from the Song of Solomon as he breathed against her neck and nibbled her ear. His voice, low and husky, felt like velvet caressing her skin, sending her nerve endings humming.

"Oh!" Her breath caught at the stark sincerity of his declaration of love. She felt herself blushing with shy pleasure.

" 'You have ravished my heart, my sister, my bride.' " Joel's rich baritone voice wrapped a protective cocoon around her. *This is real,* she told herself, to the drum of her quickened heartbeat. *I am loved. He loves me. His love is rock-sure, unshakable.*

In one moment, thoughts of the long drive and the crummy weather fled like snowflakes before a gust of wind. Everything faded except the warmth of her husband's arms. She loved the solid hardness of his body and the strength of those arms. She inhaled his comforting, familiar smell. This was where she belonged—where she'd always belonged. She'd come home when she'd married Joel.

Instinctively, following the ancient dance of love, she responded. In one fluid motion, Val rose, turned, and melted into Joel's embrace. The top of her head was level with his chin. Eyes of summer blue sky met eyes of deep ocean green. His broad hands splayed against her back, drawing her closer against the softness of his sweater.

She cocked her head upward. In the golden pool of light shed by her desk lamp, she could see the heartrending tenderness of his gaze. Love for him washed over her. Yet. . .she could see concern furrowing the brow of his dear face. He was looking at her thoughtfully. *Maybe I should cancel, if he's so worried.*

But her thoughts trailed off as he lowered his mouth to hers. . . .

❧

"Yikes!" Tess McGowen yelped as she barreled into Joel's office with a stack of papers only to find herself interrupting a tender moment between the assistant pastor and his wife. "Excuse me!"

Val jumped backward, bumping into her chair and sending it clattering to the floor. "Tess!" she cried, one hand flying to her mouth. "Oh. . ."

Joel, red-faced, spun around to face his assistant. Tess was a pixie of a woman with shoulder-length black hair that gleamed like sleek ebony. She'd been Val's college roommate and, later, her maid of honor.

"Uh. . .no problem, Tess," Joel stammered, scrubbing his chin with his right hand. "Val and I were just. . .uh, discussing. . .her lecture."

Tess hid her smile. She and the rest of the church staff would have to be blind not to see the fire that burned between these two lovebirds. "Here are the seminar registration forms you asked for, Joel," she said, trying to sound businesslike as she plunked the papers on Joel's crowded desk.

"Oh, thanks, Tess," said Joel. "I. . .uh, needed those."

"You're welcome." Tess leaned her head to one side.

"Val, do you need any help getting ready for your talk? Copies made, or something?"

Val looked from Tess to Joel. Her emotions churned. She wanted to stay, but duty called. And, yet, was she being foolish to attempt the trip in this weather? "Oh, I don't know, Tess," she muttered. "Joel tells me I shouldn't go. He predicts a storm."

"Right," added Joel. "An Alberta Clipper system from Canada, no less. Two feet of snow by midnight. I don't want her out in that. Can you blame me?"

"I'll be home before dinner," protested Val. "I'll beat the storm."

Joel jerked his head toward the window. "It's started already."

Tess's dark brows knit. Looking puzzled, she twisted one of her dangling silver turquoise earrings around her forefinger. "That's not what I just heard on the radio. The weather people say the storm's a bust. It's not going to happen."

Val brightened. "Really?"

Joel frowned. "Really?"

"Hey, listen, you two," said Tess, balling her fists on the hips of her flowing floral skirt. "Why don't you do the sensible, scientific thing and call up the new County Snow Roads Hot Line? I've been using the service for weeks now, and it hasn't let me down yet."

Beaming, she scribbled a telephone number on a piece of paper and handed it to Joel. "Since Val's such a good journalist, she'll appreciate getting the facts. But I gotta go. See ya."

With that, Tess bounded out of the room, a flash of pastel-flowered skirt and creamy sweater. Joel laughed and gave Val's waist a squeeze. "She's a whirlwind, all right. I couldn't run the youth programs without her."

Val plucked the paper from between Joel's fingers. "Let's call and settle this one way or the other."

"Fine."

Val punched in the number and listened to the recording. Then she hit the button to repeat the message and passed the telephone to Joel. He listened, eyes narrowing. His jaw flexed. She could tell he wasn't liking what he was hearing, but he couldn't deny it.

He replaced the receiver. "Looks like Tess is right," he said heavily. "The storm is passing us by, heading south."

"And I'm traveling northwest."

"Yeah."

"So, I'll be fine."

Joel sighed. "I guess. I still don't like it, though."

Val reached up and touched his face. "You're a sweetheart to worry about me so. I promise you, I'll leave early. I'll cut the talk short and have the kids ask their questions by e-mail. You'll see, I'll be home by dinner."

The corners of Joel's mouth curved. "An e-mail question-and-answer period? That's innovative."

Val shrugged. "Move with the times, Reverend, or eat my dust."

Joel grinned. "OK, you go and I'll make dinner. I'll chop some wood for the fire. We can make S'mores. Let's make it an extraordinary evening since this is our special day. Ten months."

"I know." Val stood on her toes to deliver a quick kiss. "I'm the luckiest wife in the world to have a husband who remembers our anniversaries—not only by the year, but by the month!"

Joel rubbed his hands up and down her sweatered

arms. "Yeah, lucky kid. OK. Are you ready to go?"

"I'm ready," she said, snatching her speech off the desk and jamming it into her leather briefcase, adding a placating note. "To save time, I'll even skip the video I was planning to show."

Joel plucked her coat from the hook behind the door and held it for her. "Let's pray before you leave, Val— that God sends His angels to protect you."

"Sure."

"And, also, why don't you take my vehicle. I'd feel better with you in a Blazer 4 X 4 than a car. The gas tank is full."

Val smiled and slid into her blue quilted coat. She turned and looked at Joel. Worry filled his eyes but he managed a tight smile. "I lost you once to the cult, Val," he said softly, touching his forefinger to her chin. "I'm sorry if I come off as overprotective, but. . .I don't want to lose you again."

"I'll be careful, love of my life," she said, laying her hand along the side of the face she loved so well. "You'll never lose me again."

two

Several hours later, Val stood behind a lectern as an auditorium of teenagers clapped enthusiastically. Applause always tripped Val into awkward self consciousness, so she smiled brightly to hide her discomfort. "Thank you all for coming out on such a bad afternoon," she said into the microphone. "You've been a great audience. God bless you."

The clapping began to die down as she dropped her eyes to her notes and busied herself tidying the stack of papers. She tapped the pages against the lectern and slid them into her briefcase. She smiled out at the kids again, then stepped down from the podium. But behind her confident delivery and smart navy suit, her stomach was clenched and acidy.

She'd given this talk—or some version of it—hundreds of times, but sharing her experiences with the Children of Last Days Light never got easier. It still frightened her to think what might have happened—not only to her but to thousands of other innocent people—if Joel hadn't shown up. Val shuddered. The crazed cult leader was setting up a doomsday plan to poison the nation's water supply when Joel's rescue had averted disaster.

Joel *had* come—because he loved her. He would always come, no matter what difficulty she found herself in. She knew that now. The thought warmed her heart and brought a glow to her face.

"So long, Mrs. Bennigan! Thanks a bunch!"

The youth-group kids waved as Val hurried from the auditorium. She turned briefly and waved again, then spun around and trotted down the hallway, pulling on her coat as she went. This afternoon, she'd been able to teach three hundred youths from Cleveland and the surrounding areas about the danger of cults, their mind-manipulation and their deceptions. She felt good about what she'd been able to accomplish despite the inclement weather. The kids had listened well and asked intelligent questions. Several had promised to follow up by e-mail.

She snapped her coat shut and pulled down her woolen hat. In a way, she envied these young people. If she'd known the information she'd just given them, perhaps she wouldn't have fallen into the cult's clutches. It was one thing to read about these groups, but quite another to hear an ex-member recount her own chilling version of psychological coercion. Joel had tried to warn her—as an assistant pastor, he'd seen the havoc cults wreaked—but she'd let pride blind her. He'd been right. The cult leaders had used her guilt and emotional vulnerability about her alcoholic mother to entrap her. . . .

Val shivered as she stepped out of the warm building into the parking lot. Darkness had fallen and a bitterly cold wind had sprung up. *All that cult stuff is over for me, in the past. Christ makes all things new,* she lectured herself as she trudged across the icy blacktop. *God draws straight with crooked lines. He's already bringing good out of my experience through these lectures. I've got to trust that He's in charge and He'll never fail me, no matter how much I've messed up—even with Mother.*

Val drew her quilted coat closer. She'd experienced Christ's healing in many areas of her life, but even now she still grieved over the painful parting with her mother.

Joan Packard's mental state had deteriorated rapidly during the last few weeks of her life. At the end, she'd vented all her venom at Val. Her last words still throbbed like a fresh knife wound. "You're a failure as a daughter. I never loved you!"

Soon after uttering those words, Mrs. Packard had slipped into unconsciousness. She never spoke again.

That's in the past, Val. Forget it. Give it to the Lord. There's nothing you can do about it now anyway.

The blacktop had been sprinkled with salt, but even so, Val walked gingerly, watching for icy patches. Clutching her briefcase, she scuttled around the yellow buses that had ferried kids from other churches. She groaned when she spotted the sheet of snow covering Joel's Blazer. Clearing it off would take time and she just wanted to get home, out of this weather.

Val walked faster, wondering if the ice scraper was in the glove compartment or lost under one of the seats. One hasty misplaced step on the ice, and her feet shot out from under her. Panicked, arms flailing, Val struggled to regain her footing but took a nosedive and plummeted forward. Trying to break her fall, she landed heavily on her right hand. Val wasn't one to curse, but right now she was sorely tempted. Instead, she settled for a loud "Ouch!" then "Rats! Rats! Double rats!"

But no one was around to hear or to help. Since she'd left the meeting early, the others were still inside, discussing her lecture in small groups and reading her handouts. She scrambled to her feet, brushing off the snow as best she could. Even inside her gloves, the palms of her hands stung. Ice particles dug into her knees where her hose had ripped.

"Rats!"

Val snatched up her purse and briefcase, thankful that at least her papers hadn't scattered, and cautiously picked her way over to the Blazer. Standing on her toes, she used her glove to brush the snow from the windshield. But the thin, ice-crusted layer fought back, catching the wool and snagging it. Frustrated, she unlocked the driver's door, threw her briefcase on the floor of the passenger side and groped under the seat for the ice scraper. Her fingers found the plastic handle.

Hurriedly, she worked the wedge of the scraper back and forth across the windshield, using her left hand because her right wrist had begun to throb. The dull ache was growing stronger. Had she sprained it? Probably. She could feel the swelling. Briefly, she considered going back into the church to find an elastic bandage in the first aid kit. But the snow was getting heavier. She couldn't afford the time. She needed to hit the road— soon—before the weather got any worse.

Despite the frigid wind careening across the parking lot, she scraped furiously, her breath pluming as she labored. Finally the windshield was clear enough to see through. She clambered into the vehicle, started the engine, and turned the heat to high. Shivering violently, she stomped her feet. Even inside her fur-lined boots, her toes were numb. Maybe she could persuade Joel to move to Florida!

Quit complaining! she scolded. *You've got the most wonderful husband in the world, even if he thrives in sub-zero temperatures. Get used to it!*

Cold air blasted out from the vents. She waited as patiently as she could for the heat to kick in so she could warm up and stop shivering before the drive home. Her lips felt dry from the wind, so she reached into her purse for her Chapstick. But her fingertips brushed against something inside—something she hadn't put there.

She probed. A hard, narrow edge. Something made of paper.

An envelope?

She pulled out what appeared to be a greeting card and turned on the overhead light. Yes, it was a card. A pink envelope labeled with Joel's neat printing: *To My Val.* That man! He never ceased to surprise and amaze her. Quickly, she tore the envelope open. The card was beautiful, all red roses and lacy hearts, like a Victorian valentine. But this card was an anniversary card, like nine others before it.

Ten months today, lady, he'd written inside. *Ten months of love and happiness. I'm not much good at poetry, but here goes:*

> *Roses are red, violets are blue,*
> * If I had to do it over*
> *Val, I'd still marry you.*

Val stopped to blink back the tears clouding her vision. She swallowed hard against a lump in her throat.

Hot air began pumping over her feet, somewhat reviving her.

Her vision cleared and she read on:

> *What I'm trying to say, Val, is that I'd marry*
> * you all over again.*

> *Joel*

Val leaned her head back against the headrest and tried to absorb his words. Marry her all over again? That would be the ultimate proof of any married love. After the novelty and honeymoon exuberance had worn off, after the vows—"in sickness and in health, in good times and in bad, for richer or for poorer"—had been tested in the furnace of everyday living. . . .

I'd marry you all over again. She could almost hear Joel's voice.

He would, too. She believed him. Tears welled up in her eyes again.

I am my beloved's and my beloved is mine. . .You have ravished my heart.

How she loved him!

Suddenly she had to get home right away, out of this bleak cold. She wanted to see Joel's face light up when she drove in. Feel the warmth of his arms. Enjoy him and their cozy home and the dinner he'd cooked and the fire he'd made. She wasn't much of a cook, but Joel could whip up a mean lasagna. And, of course, he would insist on doctoring this sprained wrist.

Oh, Joel, I can't wait to get home to you!

She dashed the tears from her eyes, snapped off the overhead light, and threw the Blazer into first gear. The dashboard clock said 5:35. Her headlights cut a path through the dark like silver swords, and she noticed that the snow was falling more heavily now. But the road crews had kept the highway clear on her way from Kent, so she felt confident that the roads would still be passable. If so, she could be home in about ninety minutes. She eased the Blazer into the downtown Cleveland traffic. Traffic was moving slowly and steadily. Steady was a good sign. And since this squall wasn't the dreaded Alberta Clipper, the snow might soon ease up. But by the time she'd reached the edge of the city, it was whirling down faster.

Her wrist was throbbing. To distract her mind from the pain, she slipped one of Joel's gospel music CDs into the player. Soon the cab was filled with an energetic rendition of "Amazing Grace," and Val was singing along, forgetting her discomfort for the moment. Still, it was a rotten night. It would be good to get home to Joel.

Behind the curtain of music, the windshield wiper thumped a lonely tune.

♨

Joel Bennigan stood at the picture window in the living room, his hands flat against the white enamel window sill. He'd opened the blue calico curtains for a better view of the street. His large frame blocked a good chunk of the window. The three inches of snow lodged on the outer ledge of the glass was creeping upward.

He grimaced as he watched the snow swirl across the driveway and the whitened front lawn and race around the white-topped cherry tree in the middle of the yard. All along the quiet side street, streetlights glimmered yellow through the large confetti flakes. The snow chased itself along the street in small squalls. Treacherous, wind-driven snows. And that wind was growing more insistent, swelling like a playground bully. Joel had seen many winter storms, and he didn't like the looks of this one.

Not one bit.

Behind him, logs crackled and sputtered in the fireplace, warming the homey room that Val had so lovingly decorated. She favored calico blues, American maple, afghan throws, and handmade knickknacks she'd picked up at craft fairs. The fire gave off the scent of pine. Italian aromas drifted in from the kitchen. Another thirty minutes of baking would bring the lasagna to perfection.

He'd just tossed a garden salad with raspberry vinaigrette and put it in the refrigerator to chill.

Everything was going smoothly.

Except for that snow.

Joel jammed his hands into the pockets of his jeans.

The steady tattooing of sleety snow against the aluminum siding was scouring his nerves. With every passing minute, it seemed that the wind's moaning through the pines and cedars separating his property from the neighbor's was growing louder.

Val was late, even allowing generous driving time.

What if this snow wasn't a harmless interlude? What if the Alberta Clipper was actually upon them, revving up its engine for the real snowfall, causing some serious damage? The County Snow Roads Hot Line could have been wrong.

Behind him, the soft ticking of the grandfather clock acted as a constant reminder that time was passing, passing, passing. And Val was late. What if the storm hit and she got stuck out there?

Joel grabbed the phone and punched in the hot line number.

three

Heading toward Kent, Route 480 went from a six- to a four-lane highway. After the road broke free of the outskirts of Cleveland, it snaked through several rural patches between exits. By the time Val reached the third rural stretch, about halfway home, she knew she was in trouble. Deep trouble.

Several times, the swirling white of sudden downfalls had blinded her. The road crews had been through recently, judging by the high snowbanks on the shoulder, but already new snow was busy reblanketing the highway like a fussy grandmother eager to remake the bed.

Despite the light dusting promised by the County Snow Roads Hot Line, this was the worst winter storm Val had ever seen.

The tall evergreen trees beside the highway were ghostly sentinels, wind-blown and snow-laden. The thin traffic had slowed to a white crawl. After twenty miles, Val's nerves were frazzled. She grasped the steering wheel with a death grip. Spikes of pain shot through her sprained wrist, but she didn't dare relax. The Blazer's headlights barely penetrated the great gobs of snow, and she was almost on top of other vehicles before she saw them.

I should have stayed at the church. What am I going to do? I can't pull off on the shoulder. The snowbanks are too high. Next exit, I'll phone Joel and find somewhere to wait out the storm.

The problem was getting to that somewhere.

There had been no exit signs for many miles. And on this barren stretch, she didn't expect one for many more. That is, if she were even able to see it once she got there.

The Alberta Clipper must have hit after all. Val stopped the CD and turned on the radio, only to be greeted by an emergency winter storm warning. "Hey, dudes! Three feet of snow expected within the hour," said the radio announcer, too cheerily. "Expect cold, cold air rushing in from Canada, across the Great Lakes. Brr! Baby, it's cold outside!"

Irritated at his joviality, Val snapped off the radio.

Suddenly, she was seized by desperation. Unconsciously, she accelerated. An emergency warning! What if the driving became impossible? What if she got stuck out here? People died from exposure in weather like this! She couldn't stop her anxiety ricocheting into alarm. Even her breathing became harsh and labored.

A gust of wind buffeted the Blazer, forcing her to reduce her speed. Sleet glazed and reglazed the windshield. The wipers, flapping back and forth furiously, swept her field of vision, but the defroster could barely keep up.

She wanted to get home, safe, out of this savagery.

Slow and steady wins the race. Just keep going. Easy does it.

Suddenly, an eighteen-wheeler swooped down and passed on her left, blowing up a sheet of snowy sleet onto the Blazer's windshield, blinding Val. Heart pounding, she eased off the gas and held the vehicle steady so it wouldn't plow into the ditch. Whew! So far, so good. The tractor trailer disappeared into the white mists. She gulped long, calming deep breaths. *Get a grip, Val. It wasn't exactly a near-death experience. Stay cool and you'll get through this. Just keep ca—*

Suddenly, the Blazer hit an icy spot, the steering wheel almost wrenching free of Val's grip. The vehicle jerked to the right. *Don't brake in a skid!* she could hear the instructor from her winter driving class bellow. Fighting every natural instinct, she kept her foot off the brake.

But she steered away from the direction of the skid. Wrong! The vehicle spun out into the far lane, narrowly missing a minivan. Her heart seemed ready to explode. *Steer into the skid!* Val had thought that rule was dumb when she'd first heard it in class. How could such an unlikely theory work? Now it might be her only hope.

Biting her lower lip, she yanked the steering wheel to the right. *I'll hit the snowbank! Dear God, please don't let me hit the bank. I'll never get out!*

Somehow, she managed to avoid the ditch. *So. . .that instructor must have know his stuff.* The vehicle waffled a couple of times, then righted itself. Val's palms were slick with cold sweat and her heart was thumping so violently, she figured she knew what it was like to have a heart attack. She gulped for breath. *Why didn't I just stay home—like Joel wanted me to?*

Instead of crying, she got mad. Mad at the snow pelting down on her like water in a car wash. Mad at the visibility—make that *in*visibility! Mad at Ohio winter weather in general. *No way you're gonna get the better of me! No way!*

Gritting her teeth, body tense and head pounding, she held a steady course through the white-out. Her anxiety eased slightly when she found a car to follow. She'd heard about "caravanning" in such conditions—one car following the taillights of another car that was following someone else's lights, and so on. All of them hoping that the guy up front could see!

Val was never so happy to tailgate. The car in front—she couldn't tell the make—had large, square taillights. She kept her eyes fixed on those red lights and prayed they'd lead her to safety. What else could she do? If she pulled onto the shoulder, she'd be sure to run into a snowbank, get stuck, and possibly freeze before someone found her. Or she might get struck from the rear. No, stopping—however tempting—was too dangerous. The instructor had adamantly warned against it.

Her only option was to keep going.

A blast of sleet and snow hid the taillights for a moment. Val willed herself not to panic. Then the red lights peeped back into view. She was the last vehicle in line, so if she lost this guy, she'd be on her own in the white wilderness.

She'd never hated Ohio winters more.

When another gust of snow temporarily blinded her, she let her foot off the gas and gripped the steering wheel as if rigor mortis had set in. When the gust passed, the taillights were almost out of sight. But worse than that, she could feel the Blazer pulling to the right, toward the bank.

What? Not a skid!

Furiously, she tried to adjust, but the vehicle kept skirting to the side.

The right wheel must be caught in the snow. I'm drifting! I'm drifting into the ditch!

From the corner of her eye, she could see the white banks looming closer and closer to the passenger's window, like some kind of abominable snowman. Desperately, she fought the steering wheel, yanking it repeatedly to the left. It was a tug of war, and for several hundred feet, the Blazer was winning. She cried and whimpered as she jerked and pulled with all her strength, the pain of her injured wrist long eclipsed by raw panic. She could die in a snowbank, or perish of exposure trying to make it to the nearest exit.

Out of breath and sweating, hands and strained wrist screaming with pain, she gave one last yank—and won. The vehicle lurched out of the bank and back onto the road, or the white plain that Val assumed was the road.

Thank you, Lord!

But it took only a moment to realize that something was wrong. The right front end of the Blazer was tilting forward, throwing the vehicle off balance like a grocery store cart with a rickety wheel.

A flat! A *flat?* Not now!

Lightning-quick, Val reviewed her options. Drive on the rim of the tire, which would make steering even more treacherous, not to say wreck the wheel—although she didn't think Joel would mind, given the circumstances. Park the Blazer and walk, and probably freeze. Park and wait, hoping help would come before she got hit from behind, plus pray that the Good Samaritan wasn't a serial murderer or a rapist. Park and change the tire.

Of the four options, the last seemed the wisest. Change the tire and get going to the next exit and the safety of shelter in a fast-food joint. She knew the Blazer had a spare. Joel would never let her go out without one. Soon after they were married, he'd insisted on teaching her how to change a tire so she wouldn't be helpless in an emergency. At the time, she hadn't appreciated his fore-sight.

Now she did.

The red taillights were long gone, along with their illusion of security. She was alone in this eerie, white world. Val eased to a stop and pulled off the road as far as she could without plowing into a snowbank.

Leaving her emergency lights flashing, she jumped out into the swirling snow and opened the trunk. Even with gloves, it was fairly easy to unscrew the spare tire. She hoisted it, then lifted out the jack stored underneath.

With the wind howling around her, she carried the metal jack around to the front of the Blazer and placed it under the right side. She pumped it up with the foot pedal. The snow stung her eyes and skin as she used a wrench to remove the lug nuts. She could see where the tire had been punctured by a jagged steel stake, like those marking culverts alongside the road. There must have been debris in that snowbank, perhaps scraped off the road by the snowplow.

Whatever. The damage had been done. Val stood, blew the snow out of her eyes, and clapped her hands to warm them. The wheel was in rough shape, but she should take it home rather than abandon it by the side of the road. Using both hands, she rolled it to the back of the Blazer. Gasping for breath and ruining her coat in the process, she lifted the damaged tire into the vehicle.

Then she turned her attention to the spare. It was smaller than the regular tire. Fortunately, it was also round, so she would have an easier time rolling it. Mouth set in a grim line, she began maneuvering the wheel toward the front. . . .

❧

The driver of the rusty Pinto with one burned-out headlight and three bald tires was driving way too fast. But he didn't care. He'd snorted cocaine before leaving his girlfriend's house, and he was flying high and free. So high that he didn't see the woman in the blue coat until it was too late. He muttered an expletive. What was that dingbat doing on the highway in the middle of a snow-storm?

২৯

Val's head shot up. One high-beam light blinded her. Stepping backward, she raised her hand to shield her eyes.

Before she could scream, the impact hurled Val into the air. She bounced off the Blazer, her head ramming into the steel with a sickening thud. Her broken body landed in the snowbank.

Joel's face flashed across her brain.

The Pinto kept going.

Val lay in the white snow, a broken blue doll splattered with red. The Blazer's spare wheel bounced across the highway.

four

The snow fell silently. Great white flakes knitted a shroud over Val as she lay half-wedged into the snowbank, face down, eyes squeezed shut. Snow filled her mouth, nose, ears. But she wasn't cold, and she felt no pain.

The wind picked up, whipping against her legs. From somewhere, Val heard a voice, a whisper carried on the wind, clear as church bells on Christmas Eve.

The voice grew louder.

"Valerie!"

The word came from outside, yet also from within. Val had never given much thought to what dying would be like. She knew she'd die someday, and the radio and TV talk shows and tabloids were chock full of people who had died and lived to tell about it. Tunnels of light. Angelic beings. Your life flashing before your eyes in one blinding flash. She'd wondered about those stories.

Now she felt a vicious flash of heat explode inside her head and heard a booming noise like thunder next to her ear. Before she could draw a breath, she found herself speeding through a tunnel. The winged-foot journey reminded her of the roller-coaster ride Joel had cajoled her into trying the summer before. The coaster's stomach-lurching drops and dizzying ascents had terrified Val. By the time it was over, her knuckles had turned white and her fingers were stiff from clutching the safety bar. She'd also been mad as a wet hen at her thrill-loving fiancé. Joel had held her close, promising never to pressure her into anything scarier than a kiddie ride.

But here she was, hurtling through spiritual space. The tunnel was dark, and she wasn't touching the sides. To her surprise, she didn't feel alone. Another presence was traveling through the tunnel with her. Inexplicably, this presence filled Val with joy. She heard the beating of wings. The sound of a thousand doves taking flight.

Wings? Angels? My guardian angel?

As if prompted by her unspoken question, a voice liquid with love answered her internally. "I have always been your guardian, Valerie, ever since the moment of your conception when the Lord God Almighty breathed forth your living soul."

Val remembered Christ's words in the Scriptures: "See that you despise not one of these little ones, for I say unto you, that their angels in heaven always see the face of my Father."

Could this really be happening? "What–what's your name?"

"Solange."

Without having to ask, Val knew the melodic word meant "dignified" in French, even though she'd never studied that language.

"Each of God's children has great worth and dignity," the angel continued. "Through the blood of Jesus Christ, you are redeemed."

Yes! I believe!

"It was the kiss of the angels that awakened you to Truth," Solange said.

Overwhelmed with gratitude, Val felt her heart swell with love for God, the kind Father who had given her this heavenly companion. Then, abruptly, the tunnel ended and Val emerged into a land of gentle light. The light was pure, more varied and brilliant than a million rainbows. She found herself standing in wispy clouds.

Exquisite music surrounded her, celestial harmony of such sweetness it made Val want to weep. And yet, the music held all the beauty of silence. It was beauty almost beyond bearing. Somehow, Val knew the music of the Celestial Court was not only praising God but was also welcoming her home. Home to heaven, to God—her beginning and her end. At that instant, she experienced a magnificent, wild beauty far beyond her deepest longings. *How lovely is your dwelling place, O Lord God Almighty!* The sweetness of Divine Love enveloped her. Rapt with happiness, she turned to view Solange for the first time.

Val gasped.

Never had she seen such a face. Strong, full of dignity, inexpressibly kind. It contained a world of beauty. Her guardian angel was radiant. Exquisitely humble. Astonishingly glorious. Tall and stately and golden in long flowing robes that seemed woven from sunbeams.

"If you've been with me all my life," Val said, unable to hide her astonishment, "then why did I ever worry about anything?"

"Trust takes the eyes of faith, little one." Solange placed a hand on her shoulder. Complete peace flowed over Val. "Do not be afraid," the angel said and pointed toward two approaching figures. "The purpose of earthly life is to praise God, to love Him, His will, and those whom God has made. He permits difficulties to allow humans the opportunity to grow in love and faithfulness. Behold—"

Val gasped again. "Mother! Daddy!"

Joan and Marc Packard approached, gliding rather than walking, it seemed. Although Joan had died with the ravages of alcoholism marring her face and her body and mind, now she looked radiantly young and happy. Val's father, killed in the Vietnam War, walked beside his wife, full-bodied and handsome. "Mother—"

"My darling daughter," said Joan, reaching out to take Val's hands in hers. "My precious child, please forgive me. I always loved you, but I couldn't show that love. Forgive me for the pain I caused you."

Val smiled, suddenly relieved of the guilt she'd carried all her life. But before she could answer, a pulsating brightness caught her attention. Val looked beyond her mother, beyond the stone wall that suddenly appeared, to a rough-hewn cross. The rock barrier was only three feet high, but somehow, Val knew that she wasn't allowed to pass it. At least not now.

A man was hanging on the cross. A woman, her head covered by a blue mantle, stood beneath the cross. Her hands were folded in prayer. From the man came the words, "Father, forgive them for they know not what they do." The light emanating from the cross grew so bright, it stunned Val.

Christ's forgiveness. The light that blots out the darkness of sin. The Lamb of God who takes away the sins of the world!

Without hesitation, Val squeezed her mother's hands. "Of course I forgive you, Mother. I love you, too."

"Thank you," Joan whispered.

Grace healed the relationship that had brought so much pain on earth. *By His wounds we are healed*. Val looked toward the cross again, but her attention was drawn away by the urgency in her father's voice.

"Princess," he said, using his childhood pet name for her, "it's time for you to go."

Val dragged her gaze back to Marc Packard's face. She blinked. "What did you say, Daddy?"

"This isn't your time, Val," he said gently. "You've got to go back."

Val shook her head. "But I want to stay!"

"That's not God's perfect will for you, Princess."

"But why?"

Marc pointed down into the wispy clouds at their feet. The clouds parted and through the opening, Val could see herself lying bleeding in a snowbank. She recognized her blue quilted coat. She looked back at Marc, aghast. Was that really *her* body? She looked again and saw paramedics load her broken body into a medical helicopter.

"That's not me!"

"It's you, darling," her mother said softly.

Val looked through the clouds a third time, and saw her body on an operating table, chalk-pale under the harsh bright lights. Doctors and nurses milled around her. Someone was barking orders. A doctor with blood on his white coat was pressing electrical paddles against her chest to jump-start her heart. Looking at herself on the table, Val thought her body looked like a used vehicle. She felt no attachment to it, nor did she feel any desire to return to it.

"I don't want to go back!" she pleaded. "I want to stay here!"

Marc shook his head. "You must go, Princess. He needs you."

"Who? Who needs me?"

"He does." Marc Packard nodded toward a man approaching from Val's right. "Your beloved. . ."

Val stared at the man, straining to recognize him. He wore jeans and a sweater, but she couldn't make out his face.

He drew closer.

"He needs you, Princess," whispered her father as he and Joan stepped back, away from Val. "And you need him. . ."

A blast of cold wind swept the rest of Marc Packard's words away.

"It is not your time, little one," said Solange, his long, golden hair and robes fluttering in the sudden movement of air. "You have not finished the mission of your existence. But when your time does come, remember that the path to death is lined with angels. We will protect you from demons as you journey toward the wedding feast of the Lamb."

Val shuddered. Why, in this glorious place of light, did she feel an upcoming encounter with darkness? She had no wish to tangle with evil. She wanted to stay here in the land of light. Every fiber of her being ached to stay.

As she strained to make out the face of the man in the cranberry sweater, she heard her angel speak in a voice soft as down. "Love is stronger than death, Valerie. What God hath joined together, let no man put asunder."

Try as she might, Val could not recognize the man.

At her side, Solange raised his mighty arm and cried, "Who is like God! Praise be to the Lord Most High!"

The wind grew stronger, then whipped into a vortex. Val tumbled backward, dropping into the tunnel as if pulled by a vacuum. The man in the red sweater began running, calling to her. But she couldn't make out his words.

As the darkness of the tunnel enveloped her, Val realized why she couldn't recognize the man's face.

It was covered with snow.

five

The lasagna sat on the kitchen counter, as cold and unappetizing as yesterday's leftovers. The salad, tossed with cucumbers and red peppers, lay soggy in its dressing. Joel paced back and forth between the kitchen and the living room window, his ears trained for the roar of the Blazer's engine. Anxious, he popped a piece of spearmint gum into his mouth and chewed furiously. On the TV, a local weather woman was stubbornly standing out in the storm, updating the forecast. Snow encrusted her red fedora, giving it the look of a snow-spangled Christmas wreath.

"Total snowfall may reach five or six feet by midnight," she said gravely, blinking snowflakes from her eyes. "Roads are treacherous. Visibility, almost nil. Do not, I repeat—do *not* go out unless it's an emergency."

Great! Just great. Where were you when I needed you?

Joel thrust his hand through his hair. He'd already called the church in Cleveland. Val had left early as she'd promised. That was two and a half hours ago.

Two and a half hours! Even at a crawl, she should have been home by now. Unless that, is, unless. . . .

The wind howled through the yard and around the eaves of the house, then beat against the shutters, wailing like a grieving widow. Jake raked his hand through his hair again, making it stand on end. He chewed his gum harder.

It was time to call the police, the hospitals. . . .

It was time. With a sinking heart, he knew it was time. But before Joel could reach for the telephone, it rang. He snatched it out of its cradle.

"Reverend Joel Bennigan?" asked an unfamiliar voice.

"Yes." Joel's mouth was dry kindling.

"This is the Cleveland Clinic calling. I'm afraid there's been an accident. . ."

&

Robert Bennigan turned the wipers to high. "It's a mean storm, all right," he muttered as he held his Dodge Ram 4 X 4 steady in a wind that was out of control. It was getting harder and harder to see the taillights of the snowplow they were following.

At the tone in his father's voice, Joel startled out of his daze. He grimaced, then pounded his fist against his thigh. "Why? *Why* did I let her go? I should have known better!"

Robert squinted at the ghostly, sulfur-yellow plow ahead of them. "You couldn't have known. Don't blame yourself."

"But. . .a flat tire, Dad! I should have checked the tires before she left."

"You can't control everything, son. That's what makes this so hard. Something terrible has happened, and you're powerless to change it."

"Powerless," Joel echoed, not bothering to hide his anguish. He clenched his teeth, grinding them. If there was anything worse than this gnawing, sick fear, he didn't want to know about it. Yet, if he'd learned anything at all from his years in Alcoholics Anonymous, it was that every human being is ultimately powerless, his or her times and years determined by God.

Robert cleared his throat. "No matter how much you love Val, this has happened and you can't change it. We'll have to deal with reality as we find it, and have faith that God is in control."

Silently, Joel kept blaming himself, beating himself for not investing in a car phone for the Blazer. For not checking the tires. For crying out loud—he should have driven Val to Cleveland! Then this wouldn't have happened! Why had he let her go alone? Sure, he had a sermon to finish, but it could have waited.

Joel scowled at the puttering snowplow, then groaned in exasperation. "Can't that guy go any faster? We don't have all night!"

An expletive ripped from him before he could stop it. He was irritated that he hadn't succeeded in persuading Val to stay home. At the moment, he felt as if he were wading in slow motion through Jell-O, the infernal weather keeping him from getting to her bedside quickly.

Ever since the Cleveland Clinic had called saying Val had been found by an emergency road crew and flown to the Critical Care Unit, Joel had slipped into a time warp. He'd stood in the middle of the living room with the telephone receiver in his hand, staring at the white piece of plastic as if it had turned into a snake.

He'd grappled with the news, trying to absorb it, but his mind had gone numb. He replayed the scene again and again in his mind: *Sir, it appears your wife may have been hit by another vehicle while she was changing a tire. Despite the weather, we recommend you get here quickly.*

The woman on the other end of the line had clammed up when Joel had pressed for details about Val's condition. "I can't give you that information, sir. All I can tell you is that she's been critically injured. You'll have to speak to the attending physician."

Joel stared out the window of his father's pickup at the snow tumbling from the sky like gravel unloaded from a dump truck. *Why? Why wouldn't she tell me more? What if Val's fatally injured. . .dying? Dead, even? Or maimed for life? Would they tell me? What if. . . .*

Cut it out, Bennigan! Get a grip!

Ignoring his son's outburst of foul language, Robert spoke calmly. "It's safer to follow the plow, Joel. Just sit tight. I know it's slow, but at least we'll get there in one piece."

His fists balled on his thighs, Joel said nothing, but continued to glare at the storm. It was now his enemy. He eyed the snow barreling across the open fields and blocking out a cluster of gnarled and naked dogwood trees. In places, the snowbanks were walls of white flanking the road. Ohio winter weather. The weather Val hated. Joel had grown up with blizzards, had learned to shrug them off.

But what if the Ohio weather had taken Val from him?

His fists clenched tighter and his mouth settled into a grim line.

Ahead of the Ram, the snowplow's lights winked through the white curtain. As far as Joel could tell, there were no other vehicles on the road to Cleveland. All he could see was white. White. White. Whiter. The color of winter.

The color of death.

Joel couldn't close the pit of dread that yawned wide in his stomach. He'd lost Val before when she'd been investigating the cult, but he'd gotten her back.

What if he'd lost her for good this time?

મ

Robert Bennigan glanced across the cab at his son. Joel's mop of wavy hair stood on end from jamming his hand through it. A nervous habit from childhood. The father's heart ached for his son. Joel had overcome much in his thirty years—a serious football injury while in college, alcohol abuse, the wild lifestyle of a handsome young jock struggling to fill the God-shaped void in his life with all the wrong things—and people. As a father and grandfather, Robert had often seen God's mysterious ways at work. During his son's year of physical therapy, he had been forced to reflect on the fickle nature of worldly fame and glory. Joel's promising football career as the quarterback for Kent's Golden Flashers had evaporated in one vicious sack by an opposing lineman. His dreams of playing for the pros had been shattered along with his knees.

Sometime during those months, his boy—the fallen football star—had found the real Star. When Joel had finally stopped running, the Hound of Heaven had tracked him down.

Robert remembered how he and his wife had wept the day Joel had announced his plans to attend seminary. Then, after Joel had served as the assistant pastor of Faith Bible Church for several years, Robert and Millie had another cause for rejoicing. Joel had fallen in love. Val Packard, a beauty with jade green eyes and long chestnut hair, had recently come to Kent to study journalism.

A lovely girl. A blessing to have in the family.

Robert's hands tightened around the wheel as a strong wind railed against the pickup. He grimaced, feeling Joel's pain at the thought of losing Val. Robert was a man of faith, but he was also a man of practicality. A hit-and-run accident on a night like this? How badly had she been hurt? How long had his daughter-in-law been lying by the side of the road before she was found?

Robert Bennigan tugged at his mustache, his own concession to nerves.

six

At the speed of light, Val fell away from the brightness. She stretched out her arms in silent supplication to be allowed to stay, then plummeted down, down, down—backwards through the dark tunnel.

Slam!

Pain sliced through her like a meat cleaver.

She was back in her body.

Fighting the weights pinning her eyelids closed, she peered out and caught a glimpse of a black-bearded doctor lifting pancake-shaped paddles off her chest. "She's alive!" he cried, his voice resounding like a thunderclap inside her head. "We've got her back!"

A tidal wave of agony rolled over Val, ripping away her fragile hold on consciousness. Bright artificial lights beat down on her. Walls of white ceramic surrounded her. She inhaled the acrid odor of blood. Somewhere in the back of her brain, the images connected and registered. She was in an operating room.

She passed out again.

&

Joel dropped two quarters into the waiting room vending machine and punched the button for coffee—black, no sugar. In a trance, he stared at the dark, steaming liquid pouring into a paper cup decorated with sunflowers. The cheery yellow blossoms seemed out of place, absurd even, within these halls of tragedy and pain.

Winter's cold sunrise crept over the muted tans and

creams of the room. A shabby family huddled in one corner, talking quietly. Joel knew they were waiting out their son's detoxification from alcohol poisoning. A bald old man, snoring loudly, slept with his head resting against the window. A large woman in a bright floral pantsuit cranked up the TV volume again. Joel cringed. For the last hour, she'd been watching the same infomercial for a new miracle teeth whitener.

But he held his tongue. Her husband had nearly been killed in a motorbike accident. Maybe the fevered TV sales presentations and gaudy talk-show style testimonials soothed the woman's anxiety, although the constant parade of grinning endorsers with their gleaming incisors set Joel's own teeth on edge.

"Got your credit card ready?" quipped Robert Bennigan with a wink as Joel sat. "Only $29.99—and all your problems are solved. All hail to PrestoWhite!"

Joel managed a weak smile. He was glad his dad was here, that he'd answered the frantic summons to drive Joel here—to Val. Robert's steady presence eased the torture of not knowing. When they'd arrived at the hospital, they'd been shuffled over to the Neurosurgical Unit waiting room and had been waiting here for what seemed like an eternity for someone with authority to brief them on Val's condition.

Disoriented, Joel blew the steam off his coffee, noting the grounds floating on the surface. Without bothering to remove them, he took a sip. His senses registered hot and bitter and slightly gritty. He felt removed from himself, like an observer. He tried to picture Val, so pretty and taut with her almond-shaped eyes and her masses of chestnut hair. What did she look like now? He knew enough about medicine to realize that "neurosurgical" meant surgery on the brain. What had happened to his wife?

"Dad, is this real? My thinking is fuzzy, like I am dreaming."

"Hang in there, son. You're operating on automatic pilot."

Joel turned his head and studied his father's face. He saw fatigue and worry in those older blue eyes.

"It's shock," said Robert, tugging at his mustache.

"Yeah, shock—" Joel broke off as a grim-faced intern with a clipboard burst through the swinging doors.

"The Bennigan family?"

Joel leapt up, scalding his leg with coffee but hardly noticing. "That's us! Is she OK?"

The intern frowned. "Your wife has been seriously hurt, Mr. Bennigan."

"Tell me something I don't know!" Joel snapped, dismayed that both patience and civility had deserted him. The stress of the telephone call, the horrendous drive, the endless waiting suddenly erupted in anger at this hapless bearer of bad news. At that moment, Joel could understand why kings of old sometimes indulged themselves in killing the messenger.

Without looking up, the young doctor read from his chart. Joel noticed that his pale face was pitted with acne scars and his glasses were as thick as the bottom of jam jars. "Fractured skull, broken arm, shattered arm," the intern droned, "cracked ribs, numerous cuts and scalp lacerations, hemothorax, brain contusion, and intracranial hematoma."

Joel sensed the room falling away. His chest tightened. "Brain contusion? Hemo. . .what? This is my wife you're talking about! Not some case in a medical textbook!"

The intern cleared his throat. "Hemothorax refers to

blood in the chest cavity. Intracranial hematoma means blood clots on the brain."

Joel's gaze narrowed. His mouth felt dry, sandy. "On the brain?"

"Yes, sir. Dr. Silverman has evacuated the hematoma by craniotomy—"

"Eh, young man," interrupted Robert, suddenly at Joel's side, "would you be kind enough to translate that into English? My son and I are not medical students."

The intern gave the first semblance of a smile, then loosened up. "What's happened is. . .they've aspirated, eh, removed the blood clot from Mrs. Bennigan's brain. The operation was a success, but her brain is badly swollen and she's in a coma. The neurosurgeon is monitoring her intracranial pressure carefully."

"That's *success*?" Joel spluttered, his voice raw and harsh. "For the love of Mike, she's in a coma and you're saying that the operation was a success?"

"The doctors are doing everything possible to make sure she survives."

Robert put his hand on his son's forearm, steadying him.

"*Survives!*" Joel erupted. "What do you mean, *survive?* She's not going to die, do you hear me?"

There were stares from people in the room. Joel was beyond caring.

Suddenly the intern seemed absorbed in checking his chart and shuffling papers. He jammed his glasses up on his nose and stroked his chin. After several seconds, without looking at Joel, he spoke in a low voice. "Unfortunately, she'd been lying in the snowbank for some time before the road crew spotted her."

"Survives?" echoed Joel, dull and numb. He sank into

his chair, knocking over the paper coffee cup in the process. The dark liquid pooled on the tan carpet.

"Mr. Bennigan, you may want to visit the chapel," said the intern, not unkindly. "We have a chaplain on call. I'll keep you informed of your wife's condition, but for now, consider it critical."

With those words, the intern scurried away with his clipboard. A flash of white coat and swish of swinging doors, and he was gone as abruptly as he'd appeared.

Unable to meet his father's eyes, Joel leaned forward, elbows to knees, and drove his hands into his uncombed hair. He stared at the coffee stain spreading on the carpet. *Survives? What does that mean—if she survives?*

The words sounded hollow, unreal.

Surely there had to be a mistake. Was this a cruel joke? And why was the room spinning and turning black? On the edge of his consciousness, above the hoopla of the tooth whitener commercial, Joel could hear his father praying quietly.

❧

Every breath, each movement, even the weakest flutter of her eyelids, brought its own exquisite agony. But despite the pain, Val battled the blackness, struggling toward consciousness like a drowning man flailing toward the water's surface. With an earthly effort, she managed to open her eyes for one brief moment. All she could see were tubes! A forest of tubes, running into and out of her body. So many tubes and plastic bags—gurgling, dripping.

Machines beeping and flashing.

Ghostly figures in white coats poking, prodding.

And the pain! Close to unbearable. Everywhere, surrounding her, a sea of pain. She was drowning in it, choking on it as if gulping great mouthfuls of salty water.

Stunned and battered, she sank beneath the waves again.

ক

In the deepest recesses of her mind, Val ached to return to the land of gentle light where there was no suffering, no tubes, no machines. Her parents were there. God, the Blessed Trinity, the source of her being, was there. She'd even seen her angel.

That was her true home, not this valley of death.

Her angel. He'd helped her. So beautiful and strong. What was his name? Sola. . .? Solan? Sonny? Why couldn't she remember?

Already, the bright jewel had dimmed, and that loss broke her heart. Pain roared in her ears, smothering the song of the angels. *Oh, God! Why did you send me back here? Why?*

A kindly female voice slipped into her awareness. "This won't hurt a bit, dearie. 'Tis just a wee painkiller, 'tis all."

The pinprick was lost among so much pain. A drop in the ocean. Mercifully, Morpheus seized Val and dragged her down into the murky depths of oblivion.

ক

Time lost all meaning. Val knew she was alive, but beyond that knowledge, life melted and pooled, oozed and distorted in a watery blur. Now it was a sea of faces—some strangers, some disturbingly familiar— and sounds—of the machinery and the white-coated people—ebbing in and out of her consciousness.

She drifted, a small boat cut loose on a vast ocean, unable to make harbor. An eternal soul bobbing toward the shores of infinity. Her anchor was severed. She'd lost all sense of direction. The bright hospital lights beat down like the sun baking a raft in the middle of the ocean, with no land in sight.

◊

"Val, honey, God permits suffering," whispered a man, his voice like deep velvet. Close to her ear. Soft, comforting. "How we accept suffering is our gift to Him."

That voice! So kind. So full of love. Did she know that voice?

My gift to God? This is my gift to Him? My suffering and pain?

The waves tossed her boat, but she held steady. She tried to open her eyes, but didn't have the strength. The waves grew fiercer. Dizzying. They pushed her up into heightened awareness. The sun blazed down like fire. Her mouth felt parched. Frantically she groped for the identity of the speaker, trying to access, to touch her memory of this person. To match the voice with a face, if she could.

Did she know him? But before she could summon the image, the waves plunged her into another ocean of fathomless pain.

◊

How much time had passed? Hours? Months? Years?

Val had no idea.

Now the tides of pain began to recede for longer periods—long enough for her consciousness to approach the surface, but not long enough to break through to wakefulness. In those respites, snatches of memories wandered into her mind like random visitors. Her mother, still young and fresh, dressing her in a red velvet frock and taking her to see Santa Claus. The somber man from the government with the official notification of her father's death in the jungles of Vietnam, killed in the line of duty. Her mother, drunk on the sidewalks of downtown Cumberland. Her high-school English class, the day she'd won a prize for memorizing the poetry of T. S. Eliot.

"Women come and go, Speaking of Michelangelo."

The prize was two free banana splits at the local ice-cream parlor. But she'd had no one with whom to share the treat. No one wanted to be seen with the daughter of the town drunk.

❧

The curtain of pain parted long enough for Val to pry open her eyes again. She saw a nurse opening the window blinds. The older woman was painfully angular, but her eyes were sharp and dark under heavy brows. An unbuttoned white cardigan drooped from her sloping shoulders.

The blinds snapped open. Brittle light flooded the room. "Ah, sure,'tis still winter, dearie," said the nurse, "but 'tis a sunny day. About time ye woke up. A right Sleeping Beauty ye are. And himself out in the hallway, eating his heart out, waiting for ye."

Himself? In the hallway? Who?

Val was sure she heard the rustle of angel wings.

Only this time, they were departing. . . .

seven

Joel knew every scratch and scuff on the pale yellow linoleum in the hallways of the Critical Care Unit. He was familiar with every picture on the walls—all of them soothing country scenes—every creaking floorboard, each water fountain. He'd learned the names of the other patients and could identify their voices and cries. He was on a first-name basis with the nurses. For three days and most of three nights, he'd paced these hallways when he wasn't sitting, head in his hands, beside Val's bed.

He had to pace, was driven to. Sitting, waiting, watching was driving him crazy. He paced with the relentlessness of a captive lion uselessly patrolling his cage, but at least he was doing something. It gave him some illusion of control. And that helped—a little. But when he strayed too far from Val's room, some invisible cord tugged at him, and he hurried back, hoping to find her awake, sitting up in bed, waiting for him.

But always his beloved was still sleeping the peculiar twilight slumber that trapped her in some limbo between the land of the living and the abode of the dead.

Despite his own desperate prayers and the words of encouragement from both the Protestant and Catholic chaplains, each time Joel saw his wife's shattered body, he felt his hope and even his faith slipping away. *How can God be in this? Lord, how could You have let this happen? Why? What's going to happen to Val?*

He stalked the hallway, rubbing his fists against his eyes to drive away the darkness inside his head. At the snack area, he pushed two quarters into the coffee vending machine. While the brew poured, he pulled a New Testament from his back pocket and sought encouragement from the Second Letter of Paul to the Corinthians. "We are afflicted in every way, but not crushed; perplexed, but not driven to despair; persecuted, but not forsaken; struck down, but not destroyed; always carrying in the body the death of Jesus, so that the life of Jesus may also be made visible in our bodies."

Joel leaned down and pulled the cup from the machine's metal claws, splashing his hand in the process. Hand smarting, he carried the scalding coffee over to the lone table in the tiny alcove. Evening visiting hours didn't begin for another thirty minutes, and the place was deserted. Pulling out a green plastic chair, he sat and read the passage again.

Struck down, but not destroyed.

Struck down! Even the sound of the words cut him to the heart. Val—his Val—struck down like an animal by some hit-and-run driver. What if the road crew hadn't come in time? She could have bled to death in that snowbank.

Slowly, as the hours had passed, the numbness of Joel's initial shock had begun to thaw. The realization of what might have happened set in. And that realization was horrific. His mind couldn't get a grip on it. Even imagining the possibilities drained all his strength and courage.

The uncertainty of the future loomed. Maybe that was worse, if worse were possible. What if Val died in this coma? What if she never walked again? What if she'd suffered permanent brain damage?

Joel's hand tightened around the coffee cup. It began to buckle beneath his grasp. So fragile, he thought—like life, like the human brain.

What if Val had been crushed, irrevocably, like a paper cup? What then?

I take you, Valerie, for better or worse; in riches and in poverty; in sickness and in health. Before God and in the strength of Christ's love, you are my wife forever. I promise to cherish and love you all the days of my life. Only death will separate us. . . .

He'd written those words—modified from the traditional vows—while sitting with Val in the white gazebo nestled in his mother's rose garden. It had been snowing that day, but the two of them had huddled together to keep warm as they'd composed those lines. Back then, less than a year ago, the notions of "sickness" and "worse" had seemed as distant as the stars.

Joel closed his eyes. He could see Val on their wedding day, their winter wedding day. How radiant she'd looked. Her headband of raindrop pearls trimmed with fur, glimmering in the candlelight that illuminated the church. The burnished copper of her hair, reminding him of the rich reds of a Titian painting. He'd wanted to run his hands through her hair as they stood before the altar waiting for the service to begin. "This is forever," she'd whispered to him, her eyes glistening with an intensity that had turned them deep forest green.

Outside the hospital, the relentless *ee-aww* of an ambulance siren broke Joel's reverie. He sipped his coffee and stared out the window at the gathering gloom. Another ambulance, perhaps another accident victim. The weather was still treacherous, and darkness was enveloping everything in the world. Darkness. More darkness. He didn't need any more.

Suddenly, he needed to see Val. Abandoning his coffee on the table, he hurried back to her room.

❧

He stopped and leaned against the doorjamb. Nothing had changed. Every time he rushed back and saw her like this, his heart ached as if he'd been run through with a chain saw. Poor Val! His poor, poor Val! She lay helpless, unmoving, surrounded by machines and dripbags suspended from metal stands. The machines with their lights and buttons, gurgles and beeps, were testaments to life's fragility. As tenuous as a paper cup.

Joel rubbed his stubbly chin and frowned as his eyes traveled over his wife's battered body. Val's right arm and leg were in casts. Her bruised face was black and blue. Nasogastric and chest tubes and a jungle of other plastic tubing snaked in and out of her body. But worse, much worse, was the swath of bandages around her shaved head and the device stuck in her skull to measure the swelling of her brain. The bandages made her head appear grotesquely huge, like some kind of mummified space alien.

That's my wife. Joel swallowed the lump in his throat. *I shouldn't have let her go to Cleveland. Should have found some way to make her stay. Should have been with her. Where was I when she needed me?*

The human brain, Joel knew, was an awesome thing. More complex than the most sophisticated computer, endowed by God with the ability to learn and reason, to form and understand words, yet as vulnerable as a newborn baby. A hard enough knock, and it could break. Like a china vase knocked off a table and lying in pieces on the floor. Or like Humpty Dumpty, who couldn't be put back together again.

Dear God, let her be OK. I'll do anything, Lord, anything You want. Just let her be OK.

Joel folded his arms, then struck his forehead against the palm of his hand. *I'm a minister of the Gospel, for crying out loud! And here I am, trying to bargain with God. Lord, I know better! I know You're no tyrant. You don't work like that. Not a sparrow falls to the ground without Your knowing. How many times have I counseled others to trust You in the face of tragedy? Help me, Lord, to have faith in Your care. Help me to trust You for Val.*

Joel felt a light touch on his shoulder.

"We're here, son," said Millie Bennigan.

Joel spun around to face his mother and father, both somber and gray-faced. With them was Tess McGowen from church. Her arms were filled with a large arrangement of wild flowers.

"They're for when she wakes up," Tess explained.

"*If* she wakes up," mumbled Joel, feeling like a heel as soon as the words had left his mouth.

Ignoring Joel's remark, Tess stepped around him and busied herself, looking for a vase, settling for an extra water pitcher she found in the nightstand. "I said *when*, not if," she snapped, her voice brittle.

Joel looked away, ashamed.

After filling the pink plastic pitcher with water in the bathroom, Tess marched over to the window, her floral skirt swirling, to place the bouquet on the sill. The profusion of colors in the sterile room seemed to mock them with the promise of hope.

The petite young woman covered her eyes with her

hand and let out a loud wail. Joel surged across the room to her side and put one arm around her shoulder.

"I'm sorry I yelled at you," Tess sobbed, looking up at Joel, her clear brown eyes filled with tears. "But. . . don't you see? It's all my fault! If only I'd kept by big mouth closed about that stupid snow hot line, you could have persuaded her to stay home. But no, I have to be Miss Know-It-All. And just look where it's gotten Val!"

At a loss for words, Joel shot an imploring look at his mother.

"It's no one's fault," said Millie sternly. "We need to keep our courage up. We can't afford the luxury of despair, do you hear me, you two?"

Joel could tell from the fatigue lining his mother's round face that she hadn't slept much these last few days. A few stray hairs had escaped from the bun at the back of her head "I hear you, Ma."

"Your sisters are coming up later," said Millie. "And Matthew will be here tomorrow." Matthew was Joel's only brother, married and with a couple of kids.

"What would I do without my family?" asked Joel, looking from one beloved face to the other.

Robert stood behind his wife, cupping her shoulders in his broad hands. "I trust that's something you'll never have to know."

"Amen to that," said Joel as he released Tess, who was blowing her nose loudly. He pulled up a chair for his mother. Millie sat with a thud, depositing a picnic basket on the floor beside Val's bed. Every day, she'd brought a basket of sandwiches, cold cuts, fruit, and soda pop for Joel. He didn't have the heart to tell her that every bite of food gave him heartburn that wouldn't quit.

But Millie's baskets meant he seldom had to go to the

cafeteria, which was several floors away, at the other end of the building. Staying near Val's room was imperative. The doctors, especially Dr. Silverman, the neurosurgeon, had told them Val could wake up at any moment.

There was no way to tell.

Perhaps that was the hardest thing to deal with, Joel thought, looking at his comatose wife. The not knowing. The uncertainty of it all.

Tess sniffed, pushed back her shoulder-length black hair, and took the chair nearest the head of Val's bed. She patted her former roommate's hand. "Wake up, girl. We need you. Don't keep us waiting like this."

Joel closed his eyes and leaned his head back against the wall, pleading silently. *Wake up, Val. Wake up for me, baby.*

The machines hummed. The drips dripped.

Val didn't move.

Tess turned and looked at Joel. Sorrow filled her dark eyes, making them seem enormous in her pale, heart-shaped face. Her pert prettiness was marred by a smear of mascara under each eye. Without any show of embarrassment, she swiped at the tears with the back of her hand.

Joel studied her expression, trying to read her thoughts. All he could think of was that they shared a guilty secret —he and Tess. Between the two of them, they'd sealed Val's fate. Tess, through what she'd done; he, through what he'd failed to do. Despite Millie's admonition, Joel knew that he couldn't shed his sense of guilt so easily. Neither could Tess, he figured.

Tess had been a loyal friend to him and to Val during their cult troubles. Later, at the wedding, she'd been Val's maid of honor. Then she'd taken a part-time job at

Faith Bible as Joel's assistant with the youth. She was working toward her graduate degree in nursing, and the job suited her schedule, her compassionate nature, her indefatigable energy.

It was hard to witness her pain now, especially when he could think of nothing comforting or uplifting to say. Millie was so right. Guilt could undo a person and rob hope and courage. So, instead of standing there like an oversized oaf, Joel snatched up the overnight case his father had placed by the door. The case contained a change of clothes.

"Since you guys are here, I'm going to clean up," he said.

"We'll be here," said Millie.

Tess blinked, sniffed, and turned back to Val, her dangling turquoise and silver earrings glinting in the light.

eight

Joel dragged a comb through his hair, which was thick and rumpled and wouldn't lie flat. Val used to say his hair was the color of a lion's mane; it was equally unmanageable. He wet his hand under the faucet in the Critical Care Unit's family bathroom and slapped down the unruly sprigs. Then he buttoned his light blue plaid shirt, but left the collar open and tieless. Millie had ironed his black chinos, bless her heart. Millie was a one-in-a-million mom, like the woman praised in Proverbs 31. Joel had always thought that Val would be that kind of mother. . . .

If she survived long enough to be blessed with motherhood.

*If. . .*Joel shook his head.

He shoved his comb into his back pocket and swallowed against the lump tightening his throat again. Strong. He had to stay strong. He couldn't give in to the tidal wave of emotions that threatened to swamp him at every turn.

Be strong for Val's sake, man. She wouldn't want you to go to pieces.

He stopped at the nurses' desk to return the family suite key. Nurse Bridey O'Hanrahan, an ancient crone with a white cardigan perpetually hanging open from her thin shoulders, took the key, deposited it in a drawer, put her gnarled hand over his, and patted. "Dearie, don't ye know I saw yer wife come to, just for a moment, one blessed moment?" she said, her voice as raspy as a rusty hinge.

Joel nodded.

"So don't ye be killin' yourself with worry like some ignorant bogtrotter. She'll be comin' back to ye, dearie. 'Tis just a matter of time."

"I hope you're right."

"Och, 'tis seldom ol' Bridey O'Hanrahan is wrong, dearie. Instinct, if you like. She'll wake when she's good and ready, mark my words."

Joel noticed the old nurse had tears on her stubby eyelashes. He nodded and smiled, enjoying her Irish lilt. Nurse O'Hanrahan's many years in America hadn't dulled one syllable nor restrained one colorful idiom from the Old Country. Her brief admonitions were always a bright spot in his monotonous hallway wanderings.

He turned and hurried toward Val's room, hands thrust deep in his pockets, shoulders hunched. He'd been gone only fifteen minutes, but the tug was remarkable. He needed to get back. He steeled himself for the dagger-in-the-heart jolt of seeing her.

As Joel rounded the corner, he caught sight of a familiar brown jacket. Reverend Mack Tillman, Joel's senior pastor at Faith Bible, always wore his houndstooth blazer and clergy lapel pin when making hospital rounds. Joel used to rib him about his unwavering formality, but Mack would say that in times of distress when people's lives were coming apart, the least he could do was show respect by dressing well.

"Mack! Hey, wait up!"

Stocky, barrel-chested Mack Tillman turned and hot-footed it down the hall. At fifty-six, he was five years younger than Joel's father, but his hair was just as gray. His blunt features were attractively irregular. The set of his jaw spoke of the determination that had helped him build Faith Bible into one of the area's largest community churches. "Joel, how are you holding up? Any change?"

"Nothing, Mack."

The senior pastor threw his arm around Joel, and they walked together toward Val's room. "Keep the faith, brother. God isn't through with you yet."

Somehow, hearing those simple words spoken in that familiar, gravelly voice heartened Joel. Mack Tillman was a good pastor, a man of firm faith, and a port in the storm for those in trouble. Joel had watched him be there for parishioners in their times of need. In fact, Joel had modeled his own ministry on Mack's example. He wasn't ashamed to let Mack be there for him now.

"We'll get through this, Joel."

"I want to fix things, but I can't."

"Of course you want to. That's what we men are all about—fixing things. Leaky faucets, broken cars, busted pipes. It's how the Good Lord made us. In all my years of visiting hospitals, I've seen husbands suffer more from their helplessness than from almost anything. When my Doris had cancer, I almost went crazy—not being able to fix it."

Mack's wife had died fifteen years ago, before Joel's tenure at Faith Bible. "I guess you've been down this road, Mack."

"Yep, and I'm not saying I handled it well or that I have any surefire answers. But it helps to know what's going on inside when you feel like you've been through the clothes dryer a cycle or two."

"You can say that again."

Before they turned into Val's room, Mack stopped. He placed his hands on Joel's shoulders and looked him in the eye. "The only thing I can tell you is that, no matter what happens, the only way to the other side is to go *through* the fear, pain, and grief—not around it. There are no shortcuts."

Joel nodded. He needed to hear this—as hard as it was.

Mack raised one shaggy eyebrow. "Try to see things through the eyes of faith. We come from God and we go back to God. What happens to us on our way home, God allows for our good. All things work for good, if we love Him."

"Even this," said Joel dryly.

"Even this."

Joel fell silent for a moment. "Sometimes it's not easy to see things through the eyes of faith. But maybe, in the long run, that's the only way to deal with tragedy."

Mack patted Joel's shoulder. "Listen, pal, I'm sorry this happened, but I'm glad you're holding up as well as you are. If and when you need to talk, I'm ready to listen. And, for once, I won't preach. Deal?"

"Deal."

&

Dr. Silverman was making his rounds when Joel and Mack walked into Val's room. He was hovering over Val's bandaged head, reading the device that measured her intracranial pressure. Millie, Robert, and Tess were sitting or standing in heavy silence. Joel felt a cold knot form in his stomach. He stayed near the door while Mack positioned himself at the foot of the bed.

The doctor looked up. His face had a hangdog look,

but his hazel eyes were the kindest eyes Joel had ever seen. "Ah, Mr. Bennigan, I'm glad you're here. There seems to be a reduction in the swelling in your wife's brain."

Joel moistened his lips. "And that's good, right?"

The doctor straightened himself. Short and squat, he wasn't much taller than Tess. His black hair, combed straight back from his forehead, gave him a faintly seal-like look. He spoke, as always, in a patient, courteous tone. "Yes, it's a good sign."

Lord, I could do with more than a sign right now.

Millie sat ramrod straight, her hands folded in her lap. "It's better than nothing, son."

"Right," said Joel, trying to sound more positive than he felt.

The doctor made a notation on Val's chart. Joel turned toward his mother. "Thanks for ironing my pants, Ma—"

Just then, with the suddenness of a flash flood, Tess jumped to her feet. She shrieked. "Look! Look!" she cried, jabbing her forefinger toward Val. "She's awake!"

Joel swung around, his jaw dropped.

Val's eyes were open. She was looking at him.

"Val!" he breathed in a broken whisper. "Thank God!"

Val stared wordlessly. Puzzlement clouded her features. Then fear. Her eyes grew wide until Joel could see the whites. She breathed in quick, shallow gasps.

"Hey, Val, it's me!" Joel advanced toward the bed.

She opened her mouth—to speak? But all that emerged was a primal scream.

"Mr. Bennigan, please, don't—"Dr. Silverman began.

But Joel didn't hear the doctor, didn't notice the look of alarm on the man's smooth face.

"Val, honey, it's me!" Joel pushed on, moving closer to the bed, trying to smile.

She screamed again, her pitch soaring several decibels. Loud, then louder still. Her frantic, panicked cries echoed around the small room, the terror of it piercing Joel to the bone. The flesh crawled on the nape of his neck. His stomach clamped down painfully on his wife's fear. He didn't recognize these cries. There was something inhuman about them, like a ghastly soundtrack from some bad movie or the sounds of an animal in agony.

She wailed uncontrollably, shrieks of despair, her bruised face contorting. In pain? In terror? Panic? Joel couldn't tell. Intuitively, he just wanted to hold her, to tell her he was here, to make everything all right again, as if he were comforting a child in the clutches of a nightmare. He started forward again, but Dr. Silverman put up his hand.

"She's frightened," the doctor said. "And probably disoriented and agitated. She may think you'll hurt her."

Joel cringed. Hurt her? Hurt his own dear heart? Didn't Val know he would rather die than hurt her? But he obeyed the doctor and stood by, helpless, clasping and unclasping his fists. He felt the steadying weight of Robert's hand on his shoulder. Heard Millie's muffled sob.

At that moment Tess bolted out the door in tears.

What now? Joel bit his lower lip and stared at his wife, dumfounded.

He wasn't prepared for the seizure.

Val's eyes rolled back in her head. Her body trembled, jerked, writhed, then convulsed. Flecks of white foam spewed out of her mouth. Dr. Silverman punched the alarm button beside her bed. A cloud of white-coated medical personnel descended on the room. Several nurses held Val down, pinning her to the bed.

Bedlam ensued.

Joel and company were pushed out into the hallway.

Shaken, he leaned against the wall across from Val's room, listening to the commotion. He shut his eyes against the screams spiraling into a child's bawling, then ebbing away into brokenhearted whimpering. Joel buried his face in his hands and gulped for air. He'd never witnessed such distress, such sheer, black despair.

What was happening to his wife?

Was she going to die?

He felt as if were back on the football field, after he'd been sacked by his opponent. Kicked in the gut. Winded. His heart throbbing. His breath coming in ragged, excruciating bursts. His knees shattered and gone from under him.

Oh, God! Save my wife! How can I live without her? Please, please don't take her from me!

More whimpering.

Then, suddenly, silence. Bleak, bottomless silence. Val's cries had stopped.

Joel's eyes snapped open. He glanced at the stricken faces of his parents and his friend. They looked as helpless as he felt. He slouched and slid to the floor, unable to stand. Did this quietness signal hope or despair?

The silence was now as oppressive as the screams.

⤂

Hours later, Val emerged from the sedative.

This time, she was calm.

Only Joel and Dr. Silverman were in the room. The

fewer the people, the doctor said, the less chance of hysteria.

"Val?" Joel asked tentatively.

She blinked and looked through him, silent as a statue in a graveyard.

Joel held back while Dr. Silverman took charge. The doctor immediately pulled a small flashlight from his pocket and shone it in Val's left eye, checking her pupil. "There, now look at the light. Yes, that's it. Now to the left. Good. Good."

Val stared into the doctor's face. "You're not Jesus!"

Dr. Silverman laughed. "Definitely not. Not even an angel, I'm afraid."

Val frowned, looked annoyed. "Who are you then? Why am I here?"

"I'm Dr. Silverman, a neurosurgeon at Cleveland Clinic Hospital. You were hit by a car. You've been in a coma for three days. Now, can you raise your left hand?"

Val complied, lifting her hand two feet off the bed. "Ow! Everything hurts! I'm not dead, am I?"

"You're very much alive, Mrs. Bennigan, much to your family's relief." Dr. Silverman picked up Val's wrist to take her pulse.

"Mrs. Bennigan?" Val said slowly. Her voice, although quiet, held an ominous quality. "Who's *she?*"

"Why, *you* are. You're Mrs. Bennigan."

"I am not!"

Still holding Val's wrist, Dr. Silverman shot Joel a compassionate glance. Confused, Joel wondered what was going on. Why didn't Val know him or her own name? Was she groggy from the medication, disoriented. . .what?

"Where were you born?" Dr. Silverman probed.

"Cumberland, Maryland."

"And where do you live?"

"Western Maryland, of course. I'm a journalist for the *Cumberland Times-News*.

Dr. Silverman dipped his head slightly and managed to look more hangdog than ever. "Can you tell me who is the president of the United States?"

"George Bush. I voted for him."

Joel watched, bewildered. This was unreal. Val was caught in some kind of time warp, putting her back at least two years ago, before she had moved to Kent. *Snap out of it, Val. Come back to the present, my love.*

Dr. Silverman placed Val's hand on the bed and patted it, a fatherly gesture. "Can you tell me your full name?"

Her tone became combative. "Of course I can tell you my name! Do you think I've lost my mind? I'm Valerie Ann Packard."

"And who is your husband, Valerie?"

She looked indignant. "Is this some kind of joke? I'm not married!"

Dr. Silverman bowed his head for a moment, then glanced up at Joel, shaking his head slowly.

With a thud, Joel's back hit the wall, his palms flat against the cool surface. He couldn't believe, would not believe, what he was hearing. "Val, sweetheart, what are you saying?"

Behind the bruises and cuts, from under the mantle of white bandages, Val squinted at him. Their eyes met, and cold shock rammed into Joel's gut. The blank look on her face told him that, as far as she was concerned, she was looking at a stranger.

He cocked his head, studying her uncertainly. *Remember me, Val. Please, remember who I am. . .who we are.*

"Hey, you!" she demanded loudly.

Joel flinched at her harsh tone. Val, his Val, had never spoken to him like that.

She regarded him quizzically for a moment. Then her expression hardened into annoyance. "Yeah, you in the blue shirt, holding up the wall. Why are you calling me sweetheart? Who do you think you are? I've never seen you before in my life!"

Joel swallowed hard, turned, and left the room.

He was walking away from his life. He'd lost her. She was gone from him as surely as if she'd stopped breathing and the machines had measured a flat line. Gone. Was a man's wife still his wife, even when she couldn't recognize him?

He stood in the middle of the hallway and rammed his hand through his hair. Crazed grief welled up, pulsing, exploding to the top like an emotional Mount St. Helen. *She doesn't know me! God, help us! What use is it to have her back in body but not in mind? What am I supposed to do now?*

Suddenly Joel was back on the football field. A billion volts of electricity coursed through him. He was running for his life, hot adrenaline crackling and raging, bolting for a touchdown with five huge defensive linemen in his way. Now, unknown to his wife, blind with hurt that erupted into molten anger, Joel sprinted down the hospital hallway and kicked a steel trash can standing near the snack alcove.

Boom! Crash!

"Agggggh!" His yell echoed like a war cry.

The metallic din of the steel container reverberated with the racket of a firecracker in a tin can. The lid bounced away and nearly crashed into Nurse O'Hanrahan's bony legs as she hurried unsteadily around the corner. Her white cardigan fell from her shoulders to the floor. "Be dad! And what's all this hullabaloo?"

Joel's boot connected with the can, denting the side. He kicked again, harder. The can surrendered and regurgitated paper cups, crumpled potato chip bags, candy and gum wrappers, and empty Coke cans onto the yellow linoleum.

"Mr. Bennigan, ye'll stop this nonsense!" Nurse O'Hanrahan stood with her arms folded, glaring at Joel from beneath thick brows.

Joel beat his fists, then his head, against the wall.

"Stop that destruction right this instant, Mr. Benningan . . .or I'll have to report ye to Security. Have ye lost yer mind completely?"

"No. . .but my wife has lost hers."

One more ferocious, clanging kick. The battered trash can rolled down the hall. His strange rage spent, Joel backed up against the wall and slid down to the floor. He covered his head with his arms and wished he were somewhere else, someone else, far, far away. Another world, maybe.

"What's the matter then?" asked the nurse as she marched over, picked up the trash can, and placed it upright. "Och, ye're a good lad. Sure, and haven't I watched ye pace these halls just waitin' fer yer wife to come to? Now what ails ye?"

Joel looked up but no words would come. He stared into the nurse's tired blue eyes. It took all the effort in him to throw out the words. "She doesn't recognize me. I'm a stranger to her."

The blue eyes narrowed. "So ye run, do ye?"

Joel groaned. His gaze fell to the glossy yellow floor.

"Now tell me this. Just how far were ye thinking of runnin'? To Tipperary?"

"Don't you understand? My wife doesn't know me!"

"Aye, I understand, all right. I understand ye can't run from what ye don't want to face if ye do, ye'll be runnin' all yer life. Now, I'm sorry for yer troubles, but ye've got to get up and be a man."

"But—"

The nurse jerked her head in the direction of Val's room. "Quit yer whining and get back in that room with that woman ye promised before Almighty God to have and to hold until death. The lass isn't dead yet."

Joel stared at Bridey O'Hanrahan, standing there with her fists planted on her hips, a look on her wrinkled face that would wither a flower, if not an entire rosebush.

He got the message.

Love binds.

And he was bound.

Feeling like a dolt, he swiped up a handful of the candy wrappers and got to his feet. Nurse O'Hanrahan snorted and pushed him away. "Leave that be! Now get going! Whether or not she remembers ye, she needs ye."

Joel dropped the wrappers and impulsively hugged the old woman, much to her consternation. He snatched up her cardigan from the floor and thrust it into her hands, then wordlessly, he turned and loped toward Val. His thundering footsteps filled the hallway.

Heart pounding, he reached the doorway of Val's room, stopped, and drew in a deep breath. Behind the door, he could hear Dr. Silverman talking softly. Val was answering the doctor, but her voice was low and Joel couldn't make out her words.

He smoothed back his hair with a couple of swift
strokes, then strode into the room to keep his wedding
vows.

nine

Stupefied from the effort it had taken to outrun winter, spring staggered across the finish line and into Ohio. Weak and anemic, reeling from the blows of ice and snowstorms, it finally broke through with its promise of warmer days.

Within the walls of the Rehab Unit, Val fought her own battle. The physical therapy room was her skirmish arena. After months of work on the exercise mat, of crawling, of striving to stand while keeping her balance, Val took her first tentative steps. Pale-faced, sweat glazing her brow, she clasped the parallel steel bars and jerked her left foot forward. Her bare feet could feel the bumps on the rubber runway. It took everything she had just to budge her right foot.

"C'mon, Val, you can do it," said Joel.

Joel. He was always here.

Gritting her teeth, Val labored to drag her right foot forward. But the foot was made of lead. Her fingers bit into the cold bars.

"Try, Val! C'mon!"

She closed her eyes and hauled in a deep breath. At times, Joel's ceaseless cheerleading vexed her. This was one of those times.

"Try, Val!"

She squeezed her eyes tighter and ground her teeth. Whether it was her annoyance at Joel or merely her determination to walk again that fueled the burst of adrenaline, Val managed to heave her right foot off the floor, swing it forward a few inches, and set it down heavily. A minor miracle.

She was panting. Sweat glazed her face.

Joel clapped. "Way to go!"

Nancy, the physical therapist, joined in the applause.

"Val, hon, marvelous work!" she glowed. "Tremendous! Inch by inch, walking's a cinch!"

Val opened her eyes and grinned. She met Joel's gaze. Suddenly she felt shy. He didn't hide his admiration. Or his love. Despite his nagging, Val liked what she saw. Whether or not she remembered him, Joel Bennigan was a good man, a kind man. At times, she had to admit secretly, she was beginning to like him.

But the next day, as often happened, the tide turned.

Physical therapy went badly. The best Val could manage was to drag her right foot along behind her like a dead dog on a leash.

Joel stood about five feet in front, his hands resting on the bars. "C'mon now, Val. You can do it."

She tried. She strained. Her face flushed with the effort. Her knuckles whitened on the bars.

The right foot wouldn't respond, wouldn't move a fraction of an inch.

So she dragged it.

It was too slow. Too hard. Too shattering. Val didn't want to learn to walk again—she just wanted to walk! Something that she'd always taken for granted was now out of reach, no matter how hard she tried or how brutally she pushed herself. Closing her eyes, she forced back tears of defeat.

"I hate this!" she cried.

"You'll do better next time." Joel put his hand over

hers on the bar.

She snatched her hand away. She resented his tender touch, resented needing him so badly. But neediness made her weak, and she couldn't afford to be weak. Not when she was fighting for her life.

"Go away!" she snapped. "Leave me alone!"

Joel stepped back from the bar. His brows drew together.

Nancy lifted her head from the notes she was jotting on Val's progress chart, her large gold earrings swinging. The elegant, middle-aged black woman frowned. "What'sa matter, hon?"

"Nancy, I didn't ask for him to be here." Val jerked her head toward Joel. She could feel her temper rising unreasonably. It reared and bucked like a wild horse that she couldn't control. Frustrated with today's lack of progress, she itched to pick a fight and Joel was a good target.

Anger was so much easier than despair.

Glowering, she said, "Why don't you just get out of here, mister?"

Joel's color flared and his expression was hard to read. "Why don't I leave?" he asked, spreading his large, blunt fingers. "Would you believe I stay because I love you?"

"Why would you love me?"

"Because you're my wife."

Val looked away. Her heart was pounding. She had no answer for such a bold declaration. Joel was hurting, she could tell from his voice. Her words, her anger stung him, she knew that. Perhaps if her own pain wasn't so bad, she could afford to reach out and say she was sorry. "Just leave," she whispered, leaning heavily on the rail, not looking at him.

She heard Joel stride across the room. But his walk was a stroll, not a hurried gait. No surprise there. He was choosing to leave on his own terms. His unspoken message let her know that he was accommodating her. She was not driving him away.

"I'll be back," he announced evenly, his voice calm and firm. "I'm not giving up on us."

She didn't doubt him.

No surprises there, either.

❧

Four months later, Val had progressed far enough in her rehabilitation to visit her home—the home she couldn't remember.

"Nearly there, hon," Nancy Meyers announced as she steered her cream Taurus toward the Kent exit. "Home is just down Route 43."

Val gazed out the car window. It was June, a particularly green June. The large black locusts, hickories, and tall ailanthus trees clustered beside the highway were in leafy bloom, full of summer. For the first time in ages, Val felt glad to be alive. Her headaches were almost under control. She could walk again with a little help from a walking cane. But her right leg still dragged when she got tired.

This "home visit" with Nancy would be a chance to gauge how much more physical, occupational, and psychological therapy Val would need when she returned for good.

"Nancy, I know Joel and his family are hoping this trip will jog my memory," Val confessed. "I'm hoping it will, too. I'd like to get on with my life, knowing everything about who I am. But the only home I remember was in Cumberland."

"Well, all I can tell you is, sometimes home is where the heart is." Nancy maneuvered the car across two lanes of traffic and took the offramp. "By the way, does my driving scare you?"

"Uh, no. Not a bit."

"If you remembered your accident, it would." Nancy chuckled and drove on without speaking for a while. "Anything seem familiar to you, hon?"

Val catalogued the usual assortment of chain motels, gas stations, and fast-food joints clustered around the exit. "Nope."

"That motel over there—it's gone up since you were in the hospital."

Val shook her head. "I don't remember. It's like I've never been here before."

"Just hang in there. Something might click. And Kent is such a pretty place. They've got a lovely historical walk along the Cuyahoga River, and they've restored the old Quaker Oats factory. Folks here are really friendly. There's always some cultural event at the university, and the whole town is always invited. To tell you the truth, I wouldn't mind living in Kent myself."

The two-lane road into town curved past a large lake surrounded by an assortment of old summer cottages and newer luxury homes with well-tended lawns. Orange-sherbet tiger lilies nodded along the roadside. A private country club announced itself staidly. Within the city limits, the wooden frame houses grew closer together. Across from the high school, Standing Rock Cemetery kept silent watch over Kent's dearly departed. Val noticed a striking pink marble Celtic cross that marked a grave near the black railings.

"Nothing," she muttered under her breath as they

passed a busy Pizza Hut. "Nothing's familiar."

Nancy reach over and patted Val's arm. "I know this isn't easy, hon. We're on Main Street. Take a look at that church on the top of the hill. The yellow brick. Does it mean anything to you?"

The church was large and rambling, with a soaring spire. Nancy slowed so Val could read the sign: "Faith Bible Church, Where Faith and Community Meet." The senior pastor was listed as Reverend Mack Tillman; associate pastor. . .Reverend Joel Bennigan.

In the distance a train moaned.

Val looked away, blinking back the tears misting her eyes. "No," she whispered. "I don't remember anything."

They drove on in silence. Nancy navigated through a network of side streets, many lined with cathedral-like deciduous trees.

"The trees are lovely," Val said.

"That's why Kent is called the Tree City. Look, here's your street."

Val glimpsed Joel at the window as Nancy pulled into the driveway of the tidy Cape Cod. With its blue shutters and the decorative cherry tree in the middle of the front lawn, the house was everything a newly married couple could want. Val stepped out of the car and hiked the strap of her purse up onto her shoulder. Petunias, impatiens, snapdragons, and tall sunflowers graced the sun-soaked flowerbeds. Someone—had it been she?—had fussed over this garden.

She nodded to Joel. He waved. His hopefulness bothered her. Well, not so much his hopefulness, but the fact that she'd probably disappoint that hope. Even through the window, she could see expectation written all over his face. He ached for her to remember him. Not that he'd said anything when he was at the Rehab Unit yesterday, but she'd seen it in those clear blue eyes. The man was as straightforward as the *TV Guide*. His craggy, angular face hid nothing.

She sighed. She hated to let him down. But she couldn't lie, could she? What she didn't remember, she didn't remember. Val took a deep breath and squared her shoulders. Leaning on her walking cane, she followed Nancy up the three concrete steps and into the house.

The interior of the Cape Cod was as cozy as the exterior promised. Feeling as awkward as a prospective buyer with a real estate agent, Val walked through the rooms, her cane tapping against the hardwood floors. The living room was a collage of calico and country blues. Someone, Val decided, was either partial to white paint or had gotten a good buy on a great deal of it. Every surface, except for the hardwood floors, was covered with high-gloss white enamel.

It was homey, all right. Right down to the lace arm covers on the blue corduroy couch. She found so much hominess a bit smothering. She thought she'd prefer a more dramatic decor—bolder colors, cleaner lines, fewer craft-show knickknacks.

Joel stood by the fireplace, arms crossed. His face was pale today, she noticed. Almost ashen. She could sense his gaze on her as she trailed Nancy into the kitchen. This room was small, obviously built during an earlier era, but the buttercup-yellow paint helped brighten it. The room was chock full of country charm. Everywhere Val looked, she saw stenciled blue ducks. There was a veritable parade of them along the top of the walls and across the yellow cupboard doors. Plates with pastoral scenes were displayed over the breakfast nook. An ornate antique shelf housed a collection of old-fashioned tins, mostly Quaker Oats.

It was all cute—a bit *too* cute for Val's current taste.

She felt Joel's presence behind her. She spun around to face him as he stood in the doorway. They stared at each other, the brittle silence suspended between them like high-voltage electrical wires.

Finally, Nancy cleared her throat. "Val didn't recognize Kent when we drove through," she said to Joel, then turned to Val. "Hon, do you recognize this house?"

Joel spoke for the first time since he'd said hello. "Do you, Val?"

The need she saw in his face almost embarrassed her. He was staring at her with such undisguised longing. If she and Joel had lived in this house as husband and wife, he'd probably carried her up those three steps and across that threshold. He'd probably kissed her in the cluttered blue living room. They'd probably shared romantic breakfasts in this yellow kitchen overrun with ducks. She wondered if Joel's thoughts were wandering along the same lines, and she felt exposed.

Abruptly, she broke eye contact. To stall for time before she hurt him, she ran her hand over the calico tablecloth. "Very country. . ."

"Val," Joel broke in, his voice strained and raw, "is there any. . .anything? Any flicker of remembrance?"

For the sake of courtesy, she looked at him. He'd cocked his head to one side, his eyes questioning, his expression tender. Her gaze fell to his crisply etched lips. Had he kissed her in this kitchen?

Perhaps he could read her thoughts, Val decided, because at that moment, he smiled an intensely intimate smile. She might have been a plain-looking teenager who'd somehow managed to land the handsomest guy in the class as her prom date, the way that smile affected her.

Eager to deflect his disturbing, too-masculine attention, she retorted, "Well, it might help me to know who decorated this place. Donna Reed?"

Immediately, she was sorry for the snide remark, but her sharp words spilled out so easily since the accident. Especially when she was nervous or frustrated. Or feeling vulnerable. *And there's nothing like losing one's memory to make a girl feel vulnerable,* she thought.

Val knew she needed to rein in her sharp tongue, tone it down. The psychologist had explained how brain trauma often made controlling moods difficult, but he'd talked about ways to cope. At the Rehabilitation Center she'd been visiting three times a week as an out-patient, she'd had access to psychological counseling.

Joel frowned, obviously puzzled. "Donna Reed? No. It was you, Val. You chose every color and every curtain. I helped with the painting, but you were the interior decorator. This was your home, and you had it looking just the way you wanted."

"I liked all this?" Val's voice rose. "All these ducks. . . and calico and country charm?"

Joel nodded with a bemused shrug. "I always thought we could do with a couple of dozen fewer ducks myself, but yeah. You loved country."

"Good grief!" Val leaned her cane against the table, pulled out a maple chair with a seat cushion made of bright blue fabric ducks, and plopped herself down. "I may have been country-time Val once, but that sure isn't me now."

Joel shrugged again.

Val's gaze locked with his. "I'm convinced we're married, Joel. You've shown me enough legal documentation to prove that several times over. But I don't think I'm the same woman I was back then."

He nodded.

"Joel, if I move back in here with you. . .it might not be easy."

"I don't care," he said softly, his mouth twisting with emotion. "I want you to come home, Val. I'll help you redecorate in art nouveau from basement to attic if that'll make this house your home."

She noticed that he was keeping his distance, standing in the kitchen doorway, arms crossed. Not once had he tried to touch her. She looked past him to the view outside the breakfast nook window. Cotton candy clouds floated in the cleanest of summer skies. Only the lonely drone of a single-engine airplane broke the stillness. *Move in and redecorate? And that will solve everything? If only life were that simple. . . .*

"OK," she said, turning back to him. She was relieved to see the tension ease from his face. Had he been afraid she'd refuse to return? Maybe. Val sat silently, absorbed in her thoughts. Troubling thoughts. Fears that she didn't want to share. Who was she? How could she go forward when she didn't know where she'd come from, at least during the past two years? Spread out in front of her was her future, an uncharted map.

❧

Joel had begun keeping a journal when he'd first reached a state of sobriety. That had been ten years ago when he'd attended Alcoholics Anonymous meetings daily, sometimes twice daily. He didn't go to nearly as many meetings anymore. Nor did he make as many entries. But, even so, his journal was still a faithful friend.

The diary was always there, a listening ear, when life got rough. During difficult times, Joel would work out his thoughts and feelings with pen and paper. Sometimes his notes were more like prayers, written cries to God about what was burdening his heart.

Burdens like the crushing loneliness of being a stranger to your wife.

At night, alone in his room, he couldn't get Val's words out of his mind. *Is this a joke or something? I'm not married!*

Joel bore the pain of those words silently. Her angry outbursts left him feeling whipped. Since the new Val had made her appearance, Joel's heart was on ice—numb, anesthetized, deadened. But he was still sure of one thing. God, the Lord Almighty, the Creator of heaven and earth and of Val and Joel Bennigan, knew what was going on and had compassion.

Lord, thank You for saving Val's life. All glory and honor to You, O Lord. I don't know how to thank You enough, but to be honest, I don't understand why you let her forget me. Still, Your ways are not my ways. All I can do is trust that somehow, Your hand is in this, bringing good out of what appears to be tragedy. Lord, in You have I put my trust, do not let me be confounded.

Without You, I can do nothing. Empower me, then, to be faithful to the sacred vows I made to Val in Your sight. Even though in many ways she's not the woman I married, she's still my wife, and I love her. Even if she can't remember making those vows, I remember. I'm accountable to keep them. In sickness and in health. For better or for worse. . . .

Only thing is, Lord, I never expected the "worse" to be so bad! Though I don't understand the harshness of the fiery trial I find myself in, I pray again, as I used to pray in AA, "Please give me the grace to accept what I can't change, to change the things I can, and the wisdom to know the difference." In Jesus' name, Amen.

ten

On a humid Saturday afternoon in July, Val came home to the blue-shuttered, white house she'd left six months previously. It was about five o'clock, and children in neon-colored helmets were racing their bikes up and down the street. Neighbors in shorts and T-shirts were out in droves, washing their cars and minivans and weeding their flowerbeds.

Joel pulled his new red Blazer into the driveway and parked in front of the garage. He killed the engine, took the key out, and turned to face Val. For a moment, his eyes searched her face. "Welcome home, Val. I've missed you."

Val swallowed hard. Since she didn't remember Joel, she couldn't say with a smidgen of honesty that *she'd* missed *him*. So she said the next best truthful thing. "I don't recognize the house. . .or anything else, but I'm glad to be here with you."

His smile was wide enough to crack the sky. "That's enough for me."

It's a beginning, thought Val. Her walking cane in one hand, she opened the door and began to climb down from the cool interior of the jeep into the sticky heat. The pink and purple impatiens spilling out of the two flowerbeds that bordered each side of the blue front door seemed to welcome her.

"Hey! Wait up! Let me help!" Joel jumped out and sprinted around to the passenger side. In one swoop, he hoisted Val into his arms and deposited her on the lawn.

"Joel! I could've managed!"

"But you could have fallen and reinjured that leg."

Like so many times in the hospital, Val found herself prickling with irritation. Sometimes Joel helped too much. *Let it go! Don't sweat the small stuff. He means well.* She took a deep breath and steadied herself. "I appreciate your help, but let me do for myself when I can, OK?"

Joel stared at her blankly, as if he hadn't a clue as to why she would refuse his help. He shrugged and nodded. "I'll do my best. But let's get you into the air-conditioning. The humidity's high today, and we wouldn't want you to overdo on your first day."

"All right. But by myself."

Using her cane as little as possible, Val walked up the brick path leading to the front door. During the past six months, her broken leg had mended and her brain had rallied to the task of relearning how to walk. Nancy and the other therapists had done wonders, but Val would still need therapy three times a week for a while. The previously broken leg still tended to drag when she was tired.

She noticed that Joel was matching his gait to her slower pace. But he didn't offer to help, not even when it took her several minutes to climb the front steps, clutching the black iron railing with a death grip. He hovered, but he didn't help. For that she was grateful.

As he put the key in the front door, Joel turned his head and beamed at her. Val's heart was pounding. Nerves. Was this how captive brides of ancient times felt as they were whisked away to the home of a husband they didn't know?

A captive bride, she mused as Joel pushed open the door, then stood back to let her enter. The analogy didn't quite fit. She'd chosen willingly to come home to Kent with Joel Bennigan. Her decision wasn't based on blind faith and certainly not on coercion. She'd in-spected the marriage license, the joint tax returns, the wedding pho-tos. They were husband and wife, no doubt about it. Somewhere in her lost two years, she'd decided to marry this broad-shouldered man with a mop of tawny hair. They were bound together in the sight of God.

Val just hoped she'd made a good decision.

Across the street, a neighbor waved. "Welcome back, Val!" the old white-haired woman called, pausing from her weeding. She shaded her eyes with one hand and held her trowel in the other. "It's good to have you home."

Val smiled and waved back.

"That's Mrs. McCuddy," whispered Joel, holding the door. "She makes the best strawberry preserves in Kent, and she likes to spread her bounty around, so be nice!"

Mocking his fake seriousness with a long face of her own, Val punched Joel on the upper arm. "What's this? I thought pastors were supposed to be hard-working and charitable, not self-seeking."

"Ah, man shall not live by bread alone, my love. He needs some strawberry jam to go on top."

Val rolled her eyes. "What have I gotten myself into?"

"Wait and see." Joel put his hand at the small of her back and guided her over the threshold into the cool interior of the house.

Joel's such a dear. Overprotective at times, but a dear. Maybe this is going to be all right, after all. Maybe. But is it possible to fall in love with someone a second time?

&

Val's cane tapped as she ambled from room to room. She took her time, drinking in every detail. Oh, the decor was crowded country, but the house had the comforting feel of a real home. Not like the house she remembered from Cumberland, where the motifs were threadbare neglect and empty booze bottles.

Joel trailed along, watching her with the kind of joyful awe that Val imagined the relatives of Lazarus lavished on their returned-from-the-dead loved one as he settled back into everyday life.

"I'm sorry I needled you about the country decor," she said, grasping the post of the banister and peered up the stairwell. Each hardwood step was covered with a rubber tread. Good. It wouldn't be so easy to slip. Silently, she thanked God again for her recovery. Two months ago, climbing stairs had seemed as impossible as sprinting up Mount Everest. Now a flight of fifteen steps might still be difficult, but not impossible.

She put her sandaled foot on the first step. There was still much healing to be done, so much progress yet to be made, she realized. Not the least of which involved her relationship with Joel. *If God can bring me back from the threshold of death, maybe, just maybe He can resurrect my forgotten marriage, too.*

Joel stood by the banister, watching her, his muscular arms folded across his maroon "Read the Book" T-shirt. If he wanted to help, he was restraining himself admirably. "No problem about the decor. We'll change it if you like. Fine by me."

Val smiled and climbed the first step. Her right leg trembled slightly, but she pushed on. "Thanks," she said. "Maybe it's something we could work on together?"

He nodded. "Whenever you're ready." After she'd managed three steps, he added, "You look a little wobbly. Are you sure you don't want any help?"

"Yes! I'm sure!" she snapped. Right away, she regretted the sharpness of her tone, but decided against saying anything more. She pursed her lips and dragged herself up one step at a time. *Not another word! Don't dig yourself in deeper.*

Silently, she continued her labored climb while, silently, Joel followed. At the top of the staircase, four rooms opened onto the square hallway. From her home visit with Nancy, Val knew the layout: master bedroom, guest room, bathroom, and a third bedroom that had been turned into an office.

Val walked through each room, familiarizing herself with the feel, the coloring of the carpets and walls, the kind of furniture. In the office, she lingered over the shelves of journalism textbooks.

"Mine?" she asked, more of a statement than a question.

"Yes. You have less than a year to go on your master's degree."

Val ran her forefinger across the books. A fine layer of dust covered them. She recalled how she'd loved her work as a cub reporter in Cumberland. It made sense that she'd go for a graduate degree, and Kent State University was well known for its fine program.

She glanced up at Joel. He was standing by the gabled window, his hands in the pockets of his jeans, studying her with that expression of his that made her stomach flip. "Eh. . .Joel, I hope I can write again."

His eyes narrowed. "What do you mean?"

"Well, I don't mean physically. I can write. I can even type, although I need to build my speed. But. . .well, journalism takes large amounts of concentration, and I don't know that I have the mental focus anymore. I can't seem to concentrate on anything for long."

His blue eyes mirrored the sky outside the window, beyond the enormous weeping willow at the back of the house. "Don't worry about it right now, Val. If the ability comes back, great. If not, we'll find some other career for you, if you want. It's who you *are* that counts, not what you *do*."

Val shot him a small, pained smile and turned to leave the room. She ran her hand along the floral-patterned wallpaper, her action a careless gesture to hide her confusion. She had gained a life, but she was also losing one.

Finally, she asked, "And this flowery wallpaper, did I choose it?"

"Yep. You picked the pattern, but I helped with the hanging."

"The interior decorator and her ever-willing assistant?"

Joel laughed. "Something like that."

As she walked into the master bedroom, Val's heart beat faster. It wasn't just the charm of the room—and it was exceptionally charming with its large antique four-poster bed covered with a handmade wedding quilt, yellow eyelet curtains on the two garret windows, yellow washed-silk wallpaper, and a deep golden-wheat carpet—but also the knowledge that she and Joel had shared this room as husband and wife.

Suddenly, she felt shy again. Shy and shaky, like a new bride. Her emotions whirled. But her discomfort peaked when she saw a woman's wedding ring—hers?—on top of Joel's bureau, right beside his hairbrush. A curious sinking melancholy gripped her. What a sad sight! A gold wedding band, once lovingly slipped on a waiting finger, now abandoned.

Or. . .waiting to be slipped on that finger again?

Her mouth went dry.

Again, she could feel Joel's eyes on her. To divert attention from the ring, Val pointed her cane toward the large pentagon-shaped fish aquarium on a stand near one window. At least two or three dozen exotic fish flashed gold and silver and blue between the colored stones and green plants. "Is that new?" she asked. "Or did I like fish?"

Joel stepped over to the tank and turned on the aquarium light. Four silver angelfish, as round and large as silver dollars, darted to the top of the water. "They're always hungry," he said, opening a small container of fish food and sprinkling a generous pinch on the water. The angelfish rushed for it.

"No, the fish are new," he continued as he capped the container. "After your first month in the hospital, I started getting chest pains. The doctor ran tests, said it was stress. He suggested getting an aquarium and watching the fish for twenty minutes each day."

Val crossed the thick carpet and inspected the fish more closely. Yes, she could see how watching these little guys could lull a person into relaxation. Just watching them dart and glide was almost hypnotic. But that Joel needed such relief from stress—stress she had caused, even though it wasn't her fault—grieved her.

"I'm sorry, Joel," she murmured, keeping her eyes fixed on the fish. The smaller ones were swimming up for dinner now. Above the hum of the aquarium pump, she could hear sounds from outside. Children being called in for the evening meal. A couple of killdeer trilling their plaintive evening vespers.

Joel's voice was low and hesitant. "Sorry. . .for what?"

He was close enough that she could smell his after-shave—clean, brisk, manly. Despite her anxiety at being alone in a bedroom with a man she hardly knew, Val found herself drawn to the vitality he radiated. She leaned closer to the fish tank, avoiding him. She rubbed her temples. Another headache was making its presence felt. More nerves. More tension. She hauled in a deep breath, then spoke. "Sorry. . .well, because you suffered chest pains and stress on account of me."

"We've both had a hard time, Val," he said quietly. "You're not to blame."

He touched her hair as tentatively as a shy teenage boy. She felt the muscles along the length of her spine tense. His hand trailed languidly through her hair and came to rest possessively between her shoulder blades. Tingles of excitement—and alarm—raced through Val.

Too much, too soon. She pulled back and stood frowning down at the toe of her sandal. "I don't know how much I can promise you, Joel. I'm, well. . .I'm just not—"

"You're not ready," he finished her sentence. Curving his forefinger under her chin, he raised her face to his. "But I'll wait for you," he added in a lower, huskier tone. "I've waited for you all my life. I can wait a little longer."

eleven

Val stood alone in the buttercup yellow kitchen.

Her kitchen.

Under the gaze of a flock of Newport Blue stenciled ducks parading across the top of each wall, she rummaged through the freezer. In all, she had counted twenty boxes of Hungry Man TV dinners—mostly Salisbury Steak with Mashed Potatoes; two dozen frozen king-sized Snickers bars; and eight single servings of chicken dumpling stew, probably from Millie Bennigan's kitchen. There were also a couple of packages of ground beef still in the original supermarket wrapping, plus a pack of turkey hot dogs and some frozen corn.

What to make for dinner?

Val stepped back from the side-by-side freezer and refrigerator, leaned on her cane, and massaged her throbbing forehead. She certainly didn't want to serve anything as ordinary as frozen TV dinners or hot dogs. Heating up Millie's stew seemed like a copout. And frozen Snickers bars hardly made for a well-balanced meal.

She sighed and closed the freezer door, although she felt like slamming it. Tired and more stressed out by the minute, she limped over to the kitchen table. A small bookcase near the table, under the pretty bay window, held a number of cookbooks. Val snatched one as she sank down into a chair. Deliberately, she picked one that looked used, figuring that maybe she had used it.

Maybe she'd hit on some recipe that she remembered, or that Joel liked.

After their close encounter by the fish tank, she'd insisted that he leave her alone to fix dinner. He'd offered to take her out to a restaurant to celebrate her homecoming, but she wanted to manage by herself on her first evening. She had to keep making progress, otherwise, she feared slipping back into the hated dependency she'd endured in the hospital and in rehab. She was her own woman, a woman with a home and a husband, and she intended to act like it.

So she'd make dinner. Something nice. By herself. Joel was outside washing his vehicle in the driveway like a dozen other husbands up and down the street. She was rustling up dinner like a dozen other wives.

Only she wasn't like any other wife, and both she and Joel knew it. Other housewives could find their cookware, plan their meals, remember their recipes. So far, Val wasn't having any success in any of those areas. The kitchen was as daunting as a foreign country where she couldn't speak the language. The terrain was unfamiliar. Nothing came naturally. But Val was determined to become the mistress of her home, and fixing dinner was her baptism by fire.

Still, it wasn't going well. She faced the cookbook with a blank stare. Page after page of glossy colored photographs of artfully designed food stared back at her. Roast leg of lamb with garlic. California meat loaf. Greek feta and black olive pie. Nothing jogged or connected in her memory. She didn't remember ever making these dishes, and what's more, she didn't think she could.

Somewhere in the depth of her soul, a tiny flame of

panic ignited and flickered. She just wanted to prepare a decent dinner for her husband, but the task seemed herculean, totally beyond her. The list of ingredients needed for each recipe was extensive and baffling. The cooking steps seemed intimidating.

What exactly did *sauté* mean? How long did one need to preheat an oven? The notion struck Val that she'd never been conversant with culinary terms. Looking back into her distant past, she couldn't recall ever being much of a cook. Heating up cans of this or that, scrambling eggs, or following the directions on a box seemed about her limit. She stared at a photograph of fricasseed duck with grilled vegetable medley, then slammed the cookbook shut. Groaning, she put her head in her hands. A splitting headache was just another recipe away. She couldn't do the simplest thing, so it seemed.

Lord, help me!

"Break down the task into manageable steps," Christine, her occupational therapist in the Rehab Unit, had told Val when she was relearning how to shower and dress. Christine had taught Val to view a task in its parts, not its whole. Showering, for example, was composed of many parts. Unfolding the towel. Turning on the water. Lathering up the shampoo. Each step was distinct and, therefore, manageable.

In fact, Christine had taken Val through the process of cooking a package of macaroni and cheese. There were six simple steps: boil the water, add macaroni, cook for ten minutes, drain, add butter and milk, then stir in the packet of cheese sauce mix. "Keep it simple," Christine had advised. "Build on small successes."

Build on small successes.

Val lurched to her feet as energetically as her tired

right leg would allow and half-hobbled, half-hurried, her wooden walking cane tapping furiously, over to the cupboards. Starting with the ones nearest the refrigerator, she searched for the one item that might save dinner. After cupboards filled with coffee mugs, drinking glasses, tinned peas, then a lazy Susan loaded with pathetically few spices, Val found what she was looking for. Boxed staples. Cake mixes. Saltine crackers.

And, yes, the promise of sweet success: Kraft Macaroni and Cheese.

Delighted, Val seized the blue and yellow box, placed it on the sunny yellow countertop, and went in search of a pot in which to boil water. Step number one.

❧

Joel held the hose steady as the jet of water sluiced over the roof of the Blazer and down the doors with a satisfying, splashing sound. The wet cherry-red paint gleamed in the fading summer sun. He wondered how Val was doing inside the house, but he held himself as steadily as he held the hose. No, he would not check up on her. She was adamant about preparing dinner by herself. He'd give her the space she needed.

But that was hard. So hard.

In the hospital, he'd endured the burden of helplessness when Val lay in the coma. But once she'd regained consciousness, he'd been active in her recovery in every way possible, even when she didn't appreciate his assistance. He'd helped the nurses turn her. He'd massaged and flexed her muscles as she worked the torturous exercises on the mat. He'd supported her trembling arms as she relearned her balance. When she finally took her first shaky steps with the walker, he stood ready to catch her if she fell.

Now, leaving her alone to fend for herself clashed with his every instinct. It felt like desertion. He wanted to protect her from harm, hardship, failure.

Joel aimed the hose at the windshield.

No! I'm not going inside! Leave her be.

During their short married life, Val had never been what anyone would call a gourmet cook, but she hadn't been a regular pot burner either. She had a small repertoire of simple meals that she rotated each week—hamburgers, chili, tuna fish casserole, Campbell's tomato soup with grilled cheese sandwiches. Nothing fancy, just plain honest food. They'd laughed together at Joel's little joke that if she ever opened up a restaurant, she could call her establishment "Val's Plain Food Palace."

Cooking three squares a day hadn't been a high priority with Val's mother. Because of Joan Packard's neglect, Val had grown up on cold cereal, McDonald's, and baked beans straight from the can. She'd considered her lack of culinary skills a deficit she'd brought into their marriage. After all, Joel had grown up with Millie, the cook to outdo all others. Millie Bennigan's spread for her large family each Sunday would impress even the most demanding newspaper food critic. Val used to promise that after she finished her master's degree, she'd take cooking classes. Joel, in turn, had always told her he loved her just as she was and was happy to eat tuna fish casserole for the rest of his life.

Oh, Lord, help her! Encourage her.

Joel turned off the hose and wiped down the jeep with a soft rag. The street was quiet now because the kids had gone inside. Across the road, Mrs. McCuddy came out to water her roses. Her garden was something out of *Home and Garden Magazine* with more flowers than

Joel could name.

Suddenly, he had an idea. A surprise for the cook.

He finished wiping down the Blazer and put the hose away. Then he sprinted across the street to talk to the white-haired lady. That was phase one of his surprise for Val. Phase two he'd execute inside the house.

৯

Val wanted to cry as she scraped the charred macaroni and cheese off the bottom of the pot. Disgusted with herself, she flung the gummed-up wooden spoon into the sink. The directions on the box hadn't specified how high to turn the heat. The glowing red electric ring was obviously too hot.

Her heart felt sick with disappointment. She had so much to learn.

Squeezing back tears, which were useless since they couldn't save the singed food, she snatched the pot from the range. Casting around for someplace to put it, she slammed it down on the butcher-block island in the middle of the kitchen. It hit the wood hard. Several pieces of yellow-orange, cheese-coated elbow pasta jumped up into the air and landed on the island, but most of the pasta remained firmly glued to the bottom of the pot.

She wiped her damp palms against her blue denim cutoffs. I'm a failure! How can I serve him this charred goo?

She winced as the door leading from the dining room opened and Joel bounded into the kitchen. In one moment, she could tell from the pained look on his face that he'd taken in the whole pitiful scenario. She turned away and leaned against the sink. Supporting herself with her hands, she clasped the stainless-steel rim and glared out the window at the weeping willow in the backyard. She tried not to weep herself. The steel felt cold under her hands. Good. Maybe it would cool her down.

"So much for dinner," she said, her teeth clenched. "I burned it."

Behind her, she heard Joel inspect the pot. A metal spoon rattled against the side. "Val, this isn't so bad. It doesn't even smell burned."

"Don't patronize me!"

"I'm not patronizing you. Look, we can salvage most of it. See, only the bottom was burned. And not that badly, either. You took the pot off the heat just in time."

She felt his hands on her shoulders, kneading the tensed muscles. With a sigh, she closed her eyes and allowed her tension to flow into his hands. *Build on small successes.* Well, taking the pot off the heat in time was a small, a minuscule success. But a success nonetheless.

Joel rubbed the palms of his hands briskly up and down her arms. "Come into the dining room. I have a surprise for you."

"A surprise?"

"Yep. And I think you'll like it."

Overcome with curiosity, Val allowed Joel to link his arm with hers and lead her across the kitchen. He opened the door into the dining room, and she stood in the doorway, gaping.

He'd set the table with a lace cloth, the good china, and two red tapered candles in crystal holders. In the middle of the oval table, which could seat six people, stood the most striking floral arrangement she'd ever seen. Blood-red roses, interspersed with bunches of small blue flowers.

"Oh, Joel!"

"A table fit for my queen," he said, ushering her over and pulling out a chair. "And if her majesty will have a seat, dinner shall be served shortly."

Val sat with a weary thud. She couldn't help laughing. Who cared about the food when the table looked this nice?

"Joel, these flowers are beautiful."

"Ah, Mrs. McCuddy's generosity strikes again." Joel plucked one of the blue flowers and showed it to her. "Do you know the name of this one?"

Val studied the tiny oval-shaped petals. Their blue was almost periwinkle. "Isn't it. . .eh, a forget-me-not?"

"Bingo!"

He leaned close and tucked the flower behind her ear, his hand lingering for a moment, cupping the side of her head. "There's a message there, if you haven't guessed," he said softly. "Don't forget me again."

His eyes were so warm, Val reached up and placed her palm against his cheek. His five o'clock shadow felt bristly beneath her hand. "I won't forget you again, Joel. I promise."

He took her hand and kissed it. "Thank you, love of my life."

"Did you always call me that?"

He shrugged. "Not enough. Not nearly enough."

Then, as if he didn't want to lose the magic of the moment by prolonging it, he released her hand and straightened up. "Dinner will now be served," he announced as properly as a British butler and then disappeared into the kitchen.

Val sat in bemused silence, touching the forget-me-not behind her ear. A couple of minutes later, Joel paraded to the table with a glass bowl of macaroni and cheese hoisted up next to his shoulder as if he were a professional waiter. He carried it so ceremoniously it could have been a boar's head on a silver charger at a medieval banquet.

"Le macaroni et la fromage," he announced. "Or, as I used to call when I was a kid, macky cheese. One of my all-time favorites."

Val's heart swelled. If love covered a multitude of sins, this man's quirky clowning could cover a multitude of ineptitudes and mistakes. And she had to admit that in the flickering candlelight, even a glass bowl of macaroni and cheese looked special.

Joel ladled a small mountain of pasta onto a gold-rimmed plate decorated with yellow roses. Val wondered if such fine china had been a wedding gift. Probably. He set it before her. He was right. It didn't smell burned.

"Thank you," she said, and smiled.

"And that's not all," he said. With a flourish, he dug in the back pocket of his jeans. "Voila, dessert!"

He laid two frozen king-sized Snicker bars on the lace tablecloth. " 'Sweets for the sweet,' I believe is how Shakespeare put it."

Val swallowed her tears with a forkful of sticky macaroni.

Maybe it was possible to fall in love a second time with a stranger who was your husband. Just maybe. . .in small, manageable steps.

≈

His bedside clock read 11:35 P.M. Joel folded his arms and paced in front of his bedroom window, a pattern he'd fallen into while Val was in the hospital. Every so often, he stopped, massaged the bridge of his nose between the thumb and knuckle of his forefinger, and gazed into the black velvet night.

Tonight, watching the fish wouldn't do much for his stress.

He needed to move, to vent his frustration.

Twenty feet away, in the guest bedroom across the hall, Val was preparing for bed. He'd made up the room before she came home because he guessed—accurately, it turned out—that she wouldn't be ready to resume their conjugal life right away.

He kept up his lonely vigil, pacing with his hands clasped behind his back.

Joel respected her reticence. Given the weird circumstances, he even admired it. Still, he found it tough to be alone in the bedroom they'd shared for ten months. His wife was so close, yet so out of reach.

He stopped long enough to uncap the fish food and toss several pinches into the aquarium. The angelfish, their long fins swirling, shot to the top. Perhaps this evening was harder for Val than for him, Joel mused as the two pale goldfish skimmed the food from the surface of the water.

What must it be like to come home to a strange house, strange husband, strange kitchen, and try to make a meal? Stressful, to say the least. Probably more like devastating. Joel couldn't imagine himself in Val's place. She'd tried so hard to control her mood swings today. And she'd done remarkably well. She was one brave, resilient, woman, something like the heroine of an adventure novel.

Still, he was a stranger to her. It hurt that his wife—flesh of his flesh and bone of his bone—didn't know him. And that she had shut him out because of her memory loss. Joel paused at the window again and stood staring up at the stars. A fat moon rested on the black ragged spears that in the daylight were graceful evergreens.

With every breath, I thank You, Lord, for saving her life. . .but I guess I'm asking, could You hurry up and finish the job? From what I've learned, almost anything could trigger Val's memory of those missing two years. A certain smell. A place. A sound. Maybe even a particular piece of music.

Lord, could you bring her memory back? It wouldn't be hard for You to engineer something. Would You? Please? Or is permanent memory loss a part of Your plan?

Joel shuddered. From where he stood, the stars suddenly looked colder, more distant. Unknown entities of pale fire whirling in unfathomable depths of space. If man couldn't even understand the physical universe, how could he presume to know the mind of God?

Lord, that couldn't be Your plan. . .

Could it?

twelve

They fought.

When they met in the kitchen for breakfast, Joel and Val fought—if not quite like cats and dogs, then at least like Rottweilers and French poodles. The argument was over the most unlikely thing—in Joel's mind anyway. Going to church. It was Sunday morning, and worshiping at Faith Bible had always been their habit. And on the Sundays that he preached, they arrived at the church at least an hour early.

Today Val adamantly, positively, absolutely refused to go. He absolutely, positively insisted. They'd been arguing for the last hour. Now she sat in her yellow terry cloth robe at the kitchen table, glowering out the bay window, and wouldn't speak to him.

"Why, Val?"

Silence.

"Everyone wants to see you." He'd already mentioned this several times, but the notion still failed to impress her.

The silence grew heavier. Even the sunrise chorus of songbirds had long since ceased. Joel's hands tightened around his coffee mug. He stood with his back to the sink, leaning against it. "Talk to me, Val. You're upset. Tell me what's the matter."

Nothing broke the quiet except the sound of his own words fading away.

Abruptly, Joel wondered if he knew anything about

103

this new Val. Maybe he knew the shallows, but he certainly didn't know the depths. More and more often he suffered the crippling loneliness he'd experienced when Val had disappeared into the Children of Last Days Light cult. The same startling, icy desolation he'd known when the cult leader's son had kidnapped her and held her hostage. History seemed to be repeating itself, even without the cult. The Val he'd known had all but disappeared, leaving him sinking into bottomless emptiness.

"Please come with me, Val."

Slowly, she swiveled toward him. Her mouth was pulled downward in annoyance. "Can't you leave me alone? Always, always pushing. Even in the Rehab Unit. Why can't you lay off harassing me into doing what I don't want to do?"

"Why don't you want to go to church?"

Her pert mouth flattened into a grim line. She tossed her uncombed hair over her shoulder. The harshness he'd heard in the hospital room crept back into her voice. "You tell me, mister, why do you want me to go with you so badly?"

"Everyone will be expecting you. There was even a notice in the church bulletin that you'd be coming home this week. What are people going to say when I show up without you? They want to see you, Val, not me!"

"Ah, and you don't want to show up alone and have to make excuses. Is that it? You want to have the little brain-damaged woman on your arm so you can save face?"

"Val! For Pete's sake, it's not like that! And you know it!"

She blew the curls out of her eyes. "Do I? How do I know it?"

Joel groaned. He wasn't getting through. "These folks

are your church family, Val. They love you!"

"Hey, you listen to me. I don't know these people. As far as I'm concerned, I've never been to this church before. How do I know I'm not just satisfying some bizarre curiosity?"

Joel looked at his watch. Twenty more minutes and they'd be late. Fortunately, Mack was preaching today. "Please, Val. The congregation cares about you. You're their assistant pastor's wife, for crying out loud."

"Is that so?" Val leaned back in the creaky Early American chair and crossed her arms. "Ever since I opened my eyes in the hospital, you've been prodding me to stand, to walk, to take my medications. I'm sick and tired of your bullying me into doing things I don't want to do, into doing things that hurt. Don't you get it? I'm not going! Deal with it!"

Joel scowled and dumped the rest of his coffee down the sink. He was down to the dregs of his patience, in spite of his good intentions to the contrary. "You're right. I don't get it. Do you mind explaining. . .if it's not too much bother?"

Val gave him a long, hard look. She tossed her head, her hair glinting fiery red in the morning sunlight. "I don't have to explain anything to you, mister!" she cried, jabbing her forefinger toward him. "Why should I? I'm not a pet to be paraded in front of a church full of strangers! I can hear the comments already, 'Look how well she's doing. My, isn't it great what they can do for the brain-damaged these days?' No, thanks! I'm not making myself into a spectacle in a freak show! Not even for you!"

They stared at each other, both rocked by the rage in her words.

Joel took a step backward, as if she'd slapped him. His clear blue gaze raked her face, studying her closely as if he'd never seen her before this moment.

"That's what this is all about, isn't it? It's all about *you*, Joel Bennigan! *Your* image. How *you* look in front of your parishioners. It's not about me or my feelings."

Running his hand through his hair, making it stand on end, Joel shook his head. "I don't understand you, Val," he said, quickly losing the battle to keep the edge out of his voice. "And I'm beginning to believe maybe I never will."

With that, he stalked out of the kitchen. His Rockport shoes whacked against the polished hardwood floor in the hallway. A few moments later, Val heard the roar of the Blazer engine being gunned to life and the squeal of tires as Joel tore down the street.

❦

The service was just starting when Joel arrived. He slipped in the side door and sat in an empty pew at the back of the large, airy sanctuary. Mack Tillman was already up at the altar, and the choir was going full tilt with one of Joel's favorite hymns, "Where Charity and Love Prevail." They sang sweetly, but Joel absorbed none of that sweetness. Bitterness, not charity, had prevailed in his house this morning.

And it was only Val's first morning home. His stomach knotted. Would things get better?

Or would they only get worse?

Joel rested his elbows on the knees of his navy chinos, his head in his hands. He loosened his tie and opened the collar of his pale blue oxford cloth shirt. The lack of charity and love wasn't all Val's fault, either. He'd let his own frustrations get the better of him. Ever since his conversion to Christ during his college years, Joel had fought against his temper. *Nice going, Bennigan. Drive her away just when she needs you most,* he admonished himself. *Lord, help me! Give me grace to overcome my weakness.*

He flexed his hands and rolled his shoulders, trying to shake off the tension, then spotted his family near the front of the traditionally styled sanctuary. The Bennigans took up an entire pew: Millie and Robert; his older brother, Matthew, and his wife, Sarah, and their two boys; his older sister, Charity; and the twins, Faith and Hope. Joel noticed that Ruthie wasn't there. Ruthie was the Bennigans' severely retarded twelve-year-old foster child. If she wasn't having a good day, Millie would leave her at home with a baby-sitter during church.

His family. A shaft of disappointment pierced Joel. Val would miss Millie's family dinner this afternoon. And, knowing Millie, she'd probably baked some special kind of cake to celebrate Val's homecoming. Poor Val. Where had she ever gotten the idea she'd be a curiosity or a spectacle?

Joel clasped and unclasped his hands, stumped by his inability to understand his wife. Maybe she just needed some space, some time to get used to the idea of the congregation caring for her. Maybe she'd come next week.

A decade ago, when Joel had joined AA, the first thing he'd learned was that he was powerless over his alcohol problem. The second thing was to take life one day at a time. The third was to turn over each problem, no matter how big or how small, to God. These principles had served him well, had become his way of life.

Turn it over. Turn it over. Turn it over.

Joel picked up the hymnal and began singing. He

would cast all his cares upon the Lord who cared for him, and he'd take things one day at a time. Even an hour at a time, if necessary.

❧

Val stood in the shower, letting the hot water wash away her tears. These mood swings! Her appalling lack of emotional control! How had she come to this? She felt ashamed of herself and her most recent outburst at Joel. Her anger just seemed to bubble up and explode like milk boiling over in a saucepan. She felt helpless against it.

But she knew—at least her mind knew—that this wasn't true. Hadn't her psychologist, a believing Christian, told her over and over that she was not at the mercy of these moods? They were a result of her head injury, Dr. Ross had explained, but she could learn to cope with them, and through God's grace and good professional help, overcome them. Or at least manage them so she didn't alienate and emotionally abuse the people around her.

Dr. Ross had explained that she needed to examine the roots of her anger. "When you feel like lashing out," he had said, "quietly ask yourself what's really bothering you. Ask God to help you see deeply into your heart— what's festering at the root of the anger? That's the issue that needs addressing. Once you know your needs, make them known to others. Don't expect people to be mind-readers, especially your husband."

She didn't have to live the life of a shrew.

She didn't have to—and she wouldn't.

At least I didn't hurl a plate at Joel and do him bodily harm. I guess I should be thankful for that.

After washing her hair with lemony shampoo, Val stepped out of the shower, dried off, and slipped into her yellow bathrobe. As she was blow-drying her hair, she followed Dr. Ross's advice and reflected prayerfully on why she'd gotten so angry at Joel. It certainly wasn't inappropriate for him to assume she'd go to church with him. In fact, she'd faithfully attended services at the hospital. Worshiping God was an important part of her life.

So her reluctance to go to church wasn't because she was losing her faith or turning her back on God. No, it was something far more practical, more gritty, more visceral, she decided as she styled her hair with a round bristle brush.

What's the real issue here? She held the hair dryer above her head and closed her eyes as the air rippled over her like a warm waterfall. Behind closed eyes, she peered deeply into her heart and saw. . .fear. *Fear?* Yes, she could feel it, taste it, see it on the face of a vulnerable young girl. Herself. Vulnerability so raw, it shocked her, as if she'd stumbled into a room and witnessed something obscene. If she went to church, she'd be walking into the midst of strangers, exposing herself, putting herself at their mercy.

And that frightened her beyond belief.

How would these people react, especially when it became painfully obvious that she didn't remember them? What then? Would they be superficially polite, but in reality scorn and reject her? Pity her? Gossip about her behind her back? Or what if they already knew about her memory loss and considered her defective?

Tears pricked Val's closed eyelids, shimmering in the corners. *I know this fear. I've felt it before. Profound insecurity. When? Where?*

Blinking away her tears, she clicked off the hair dryer. She forced back the rancid dread oozing up from her stomach and leaned against the bathroom wall, feeling

dazed. Fear. She should have known her anger was
rooted in fear. Down the corridors of memory, she heard
laughter. Ridicule. She was no stranger to the humiliation of being gossiped about, of being laughed at. Of
fingers pointing because she was different, defective,
not good enough.

A spectacle on display. A freak in a side show.

I know these feelings.

She could feel her heartbeat thunder as she relived the
humiliation of her childhood. Because of her mother's
alcoholism, Val had grown up the object of ridicule,
curiosity, and pity. All her life, she staggered under the
stigma of the daughter of the town drunk. Like mother,
like daughter, old women would say, shaking their heads.
She'd endured the scorn of the other kids at school.

The town was small, and Joan's disease was hard to
hide, especially when she'd lurched from bar to bar,
singing for drinks, sometimes trading more than her
voice for the poison she craved. It was hard to hide when
creditors pounded on the door, or when the neighbors
watched Joan and Val gather up their few pitiful belong-
ings to move to a still more dilapidated and cheaper
house.

*Oh! So that's it! No wonder I'm afraid of being an
object of curiosity.*

Val opened her eyes and looked into the eyes of the
woman in the mirror. They were almond-shaped, green
pools of tears. *It's not like that anymore,* Val, she
reminded herself sternly. *You're not a child, or a victim.
You're an adult now, and you can hold your own. No
more running scared.*

Val knew that she had managed to rise above the
town's contempt and make something of herself. She'd

graduated high school with honors, then college. After that, she'd worked hard as a journalist in the town that had once despised her and had won the people's respect, along with several writing awards.

The scared and scorned child belonged to Val's past, not to her future.

Her future? As a pastor's wife? What did that entail?

Her heart skipped a beat. What if she wasn't up to the job? She could barely cook dinner, never mind teach Sunday school and lead women's Bible studies! Again, she could almost taste her fear of failure.

Then, everything clicked. The key turned in the lock. She realized that not only was she afraid of the contempt of people at church; perhaps even more intimidating was the fear of failing them if they accepted her. Those fears were at the heart of her outburst at Joel. Justifiable, maybe. But even so, Val wanted to believe God's promise that love casts out all fear.

She placed the hair dryer on the vanity.

Did she have the courage to put God's promise to the test?

Could she answer that question? Did she dare?

Val wiped the condensation off the mirror above the sink and studied her reflection. Her face looked thin and drawn. Her skin was pale. The dark circles under her eyes gave her the look of someone who had suffered through a long illness. Hers was the face of a woman who'd been through a terrible battle.

But it wasn't the face of a loser.

By the grace of God, she was a survivor, a fighter. Turning up at church was just one more battle to be won, like the struggle to learn to walk again.

She raised her fingers to her cheek. A little makeup

would improve her color. At least her hair looked good. *Heal me, Lord, and I shall be truly healed.*

Humming a little song of victory, she left the bathroom and hustled into Joel's bedroom. She slid open the doors of the walk-in closet. As she suspected, one side was lined with women's clothing. Racks of jeans, skirts, tops, dresses. Shelves of sweaters and shoes. Purses dangling from hangers.

Although she had no recollection of them, she knew that these items belonged to her. The closet was orderly—jeans at one end, skirts at the other. The clothes were good quality and tasteful. Nothing flashy or extravagant. She rummaged through the dresses, pulling out each one for a better look, searching for something suitable. Finally, she decided on a white cotton shirtdress with small blue flowers and a wide navy and gold belt. Then she found a pair of plain white, low-heeled pumps and a soft white clutch purse.

Together, they made an outfit nice enough for church.

thirteen

Faith Bible Church is practically around the corner, Val
realized as she studied the road map. *Good. I can walk
there.* Driving a vehicle was out of the question, at least
at the moment. That was a skill that, like walking or
keyboarding, she would have to relearn.

At the kitchen table, Val copied the names of the
streets onto an index card she'd retrieved from her vir-
tually unused recipe box. She put the card in her purse
and picked up her walking cane. Although she wanted
to leave the cane behind, she figured she might need
it—even on such a short walk. A set of keys hung by
the front door. Were they hers? Or a spare? She couldn't
tell. She lifted them off the hook, and by trial and error,
found the key to the front door, locked it, and set out.

The heat hadn't reached the blistering stage yet, but the
pavement warmed the soles of Val's pumps. Throughout
the neighborhood of neat frame homes, the grass had
been baked to a brownish, straw-like crisp, despite the
water sprinklers. The trees had a wilted, weary look.
Even the butterflies fluttered sluggishly from flower to
flower.

Val hurried along the two tree-lined side streets that
led to Main Street. Consulting her index card, she turned
right. Before her, beyond the small downtown shops,
Main Street climbed uphill for about a mile. Faith Bible
stood at the top of the hill, overlooking the town. As she
recalled from her home visit with Nancy, the yellow

113

brick church was large and sprawling.

Somewhere across town, a train whistle moaned.

Did she know that sound? Had she heard it before?

She didn't remember.

Her latent frustration welled up. Why couldn't she recall even the simplest things from the past two years? Would she ever remember? Would she ever drive again, like a normal person? Would she need anti-seizure medication for the rest of her life? Would her leg always turn gimpy when she got tired? Would she ever hold a paying job again?

So many questions—and no answers.

Suppressing a small groan, Val swung right and headed toward the church. She walked at a steady, even pace, barely using her walking cane and grateful for the occasional cool breeze. The sun felt like warm oil smoothing her bare arms. The street was deserted. Apparently, on Sunday mornings, Kent was a ghost town. People were at church, in bed, or—as in the case of the fraternity houses with empty beer cans littering their yards—sleeping off hangovers.

She reached the church. It was an impressive building. Fanning herself with her purse, Val made her way through the maze of parked cars jamming Faith Bible's parking lot. The service, obviously well attended, was already underway. She stood at the heavy wooden doors and could hear the choir singing.

She put her hand on the large, black iron doorknob.

Are you ready for this?

Yes, perfect love casts out all fear.

She pushed the door open and stepped into the cool vestibule. It was empty. Everyone was in the sanctuary. She stopped to smooth her hair and was suddenly struck by a troublesome thought. What if Joel wasn't happy to see her? After her outburst this morning, would a warm welcome be too much to expect?

❧

Somewhere on the edge of consciousness, Joel heard the door behind him swish open, but he was so absorbed in the Scripture reading that he didn't look around. The prophecies of the Suffering Messiah in the book of Isaiah had always captured his imagination and fanned the flame of faith in his heart. God had shown mankind His love not only by suffering for them but also by foretelling His plan of salvation in great detail. For Joel, these prophecies were a road map that led straight to Jesus Christ.

He leaned back against the hard wooden pew, still holding his Bible open in his lap, but closing his eyes to better concentrate on Mack's reading. There was something special about hearing the Word of the Lord read aloud.

" 'By His stripes, we are healed,' " Mack read.

Joel sensed someone sitting down beside him. Then, a faint smell of lemony shampoo. Next, a gentle touch to his forearm. His eyes snapped open, and he blinked in disbelief.

"Val!" he whispered. "What are you doing here?"

"It's Sunday. I came to church."

Not caring if anyone noticed, he pulled her close and hugged her hard. Partly because he was confused by a powerful wave of joy and partly to hide the unmanly lump constricting his throat.

When Joel finally released her, Val scooted about a hand's length away, leaving a more respectable distance between them on the pew. She stared straight ahead, at a loss for words and grateful that the service precluded talking. Joel was a large man with formidable shoulders, and his crushing embrace had not only taken her by surprise, but had knocked the wind out of her. One thing for sure: he definitely wasn't unhappy to see her.

Joel was a good man, and she didn't like driving him to the brink of anger. He'd even whispered an apology about losing his temper back at the house.

She'd apologized too.

Maybe they could be friends. That was a start.

Val recognized Pastor Mack from his visits when she was in the hospital. He stood behind the simple wooden pulpit. He'd finished the Scripture reading and was beginning his sermon. Val stole a glance at Joel. He was leaning forward, broad hands clasped, concentrating on Mack's words.

Secretly, she studied Joel's profile. He was handsome in a craggy kind of way. Determined, square chin. Strong nose. His face could have belonged to a prize gladiator in the Roman Colosseum. Joel Bennigan was a fighter. She could feel it when he was close, see it in his stance, recognize it in the way he approached problems. He had overcome his own physical injuries and alcohol demons. Now he was fighting to save his marriage.

Their marriage.

Her throat tightened.

She turned her attention back to Mack and kept her gaze riveted on the pastor. *Perfect love casts out all fear,* she reminded herself. Joel said he loved her. She'd felt the depth of his emotion in his embrace. And yet. . .and yet. . .what if it was the old Val he loved so much? Could he love her as she was now? At times, she could barely stand to live with herself! How could she expect him to cherish a woman whose moods changed like the wind? A wife who couldn't return his love because she didn't remember him?

Enough! Have faith! Quit feeling sorry for yourself!

Val tried to tune into Mack's sermon and tune herself out. Mack was good. He obviously loved the Word of God and had the gift of breaking open ever deeper levels of meaning for his congregation. From the references he was using, Val figured that he'd just read Isaiah 53.

"Christ took our wounds, our infirmities upon Himself," Mack said, his face earnest. "By His stripes, we—unworthy though we are—are healed. Is there abuse in your past? Illness? Depression? Addiction? Why are we still lugging these burdens around, brothers and sisters? He has borne our griefs and carried our sorrows. Why do we insist on carrying them a second time? Listen to Jesus' words: 'Come unto me, all you who are burdened and heavy laden and I will give you rest.' That's the Lord's promise. Let's take Him at His word."

Val listened intently, questioning herself. Did she truly believe Christ's promise of healing? So much in her life was broken, tattered, in need of God's peace. She wanted to believe, to have the kind of faith that moved mountains, even mountains of alienation, hurt, and anger.

Right now, doubts hovered around her like vultures. At times, such complete healing seemed too much to hope for. It wasn't only her body that had been broken the night of the accident. She was only now realizing how badly her marriage had been wounded. And realizing how much that union, now stumbling into its second childhood, needed the healing fruits of the Holy Spirit:

patience, peace, joy. . .love.

She glanced down at her hands. Her ring finger was bare. Joel had said the hospital staff had given her wedding ring to him. She'd seen it on his bureau and knew he wanted her to wear it again. Did he know what he was asking for? Did she?

fourteen

Joel threw the Blazer into first gear and headed for the exit of Faith Bible's parking lot. The blacktop was steaming and, in places, the tar appeared soft. The sunbaked cars looked hot as ovens on wheels. Val watched the women in their pastel dresses and the men, in loosened ties, surge out of the church and stroll toward their vehicles, fanning themselves with bulletins and straw hats.

Many of them waved at her and she waved back, feeling a little like the Queen of England taking leave of her admirers. How they'd clapped when Pastor Mack had announced her return! The entire congregation had turned and feasted their eyes on her, much like wedding guests watching the bride. At that moment, Val had identified with every bride who'd ever blushed her way up the aisle. Red-faced, she'd endured their loving attention. They'd clapped wildly. Someone had even whistled. Joel himself had whooped as if he were cheering for a winning football team.

But despite her discomfort, Val had been touched, truly touched.

Perhaps the good folk of Faith Bible cared, after all, just as Joel had tried to assure her. That thought brought its own bleak shadow, however, making her feel even worse about her cutting accusations that Joel was only concerned with protecting his image. Where had she gotten *that* snide piece of nastiness? When she'd hurled it at him in the kitchen, he'd looked as startled as if she'd hauled off and slapped him across the face. She might as well have. Her words had erupted in scalding bitterness that burned and disfigured. Now that sanity had returned, the memory filled her with shame.

At least Joel had forgiven her. He'd even apologized for his own angry reaction. But how much longer could she count on his graciousness? Seventy times seven? Even a man of the cloth had his limits, surely.

She ran her fingertips over the glove-soft leather of her clutch purse and watched the passing trees and storefronts. At the outskirts of town, white frame houses stood hard-baked in the cauldron of the midday sun. In one yard, small children splashed in a pink plastic pool. In another, teenage girls sunned themselves on the grass.

But the ugly kitchen scene kept crowding out the peaceful surroundings. Val found herself blinking back tears. These mercurial moods! She hated them, hated herself for yielding to them. She hadn't always been swift to wound with words. Her memories didn't reveal an angry young woman. Joel insisted that her sharp tongue had only appeared after the accident.

So who was she now? Was she the gentle wife or the shrill shrew? Which woman was the real Val? *Who am I?* Val closed her eyes to squeeze back her emotions that threatened to roil out of control.

It frightened her to admit that she didn't know which woman was the real Val.

Somewhere deep inside, the fissure of panic that had started in the hospital yawned wider. That panic was like a parasite living in her blood. It lurked, hidden much of the time, but ready to erupt and destroy the hope of learning who she was.

What if she *never* knew?

She couldn't, wouldn't, allow her thoughts to gravitate toward that black hole. She'd only break into tears, and she wanted to look her best for Millie's Sunday dinner. "Do you mind if I turn up the air?" Joel asked, his fingers already on the slide control.

Val deliberately made her voice cheerier than her mood, editing out the darkness lapping around the edge of her spirit. "Uh. . .no. That would be nice. It's so hot today."

Joel adjusted the controls with his right hand, steering with his left. "Hot and sticky. Don't worry, weather around here doesn't get much more humid than this. We might even get a cool spell next week."

"That would be a relief." Val nodded to cover her uneasiness, then leaned her head against the neck-rest and let the cold air gushing from the dashboard vents wash over her. The chilly blast cleared her mind and soothed her turgid emotions.

A large red-brick apartment complex flashed by. Val closed her eyes and listened to Joel shift gears. Her mind wandered back to the scene at church. Immediately after the last hymn, dozens of people had descended upon her and Joel. Their pew had suddenly been jammed with bodies. Val had shaken hands. She'd smiled, tried to be gracious. But she'd been at a loss for words, especially when one teenaged girl seemed hurt that Val couldn't recall her name. Joel had seemed to sense her discomfort and had spirited her away, maintaining that they needed to get to his mother's house for dinner.

Now as they left the church farther and farther behind, Val was struck by the eerie feeling that she and Joel were actors playing a part, performing the ancient ritual of the bride and groom hurrying from the crowd of well-wishers at their wedding. Perhaps, once upon a time, they had done just that. Man and wife escaping to a new life. Fleeing toward the future. *Their* future—full of passion, pain, and promise.

Val glanced surreptitiously at her husband, the stranger she was just beginning to get to know. Joel. He was drumming his strong fingers against the steering wheel, humming the tune of a hymn. Despite his off-key warbling, Val recognized the melody of "Where Charity and Love Prevail."

Were they really a bride and groom driving toward their future? Once again? What would the future hold for them this time out of the gate? Charity? Love? Or something else?

&

Millie and Robert Bennigan lived on a rural stretch of Edison Road, ten miles outside Kent. Joel pointed out the large stone farmhouse on the rambling country estate surrounded by miles of white fence. A stand of ancient oaks framed the house. Several horses grazed on the sun-dappled grass. The pastures and woods behind the house and outbuildings stretched as far as Val could see.

"This is it," Joel announced.

"*This* is your parents' place?"

"Uh huh." Joel looped onto the gravel driveway lined with gigantic silver birches. "Be it ever so humble. I grew up here. After college and seminary, I moved back and lived in the basement apartment until. . .well, until you and I got married and moved into town."

The house had a well-preserved, sparkling look, enhanced by the gleaming fire-engine-red shutters and doors. Red geraniums overflowed from window boxes on the six downstairs windows. A black Lexus and a red minivan were parked along the curved driveway in front of the main door.

"Hey, you never told me I married into money!"

"Would it have made a difference?"

Only half serious, Val shot him a withering look.

Joel raised one hand in mock surrender. "Hey, just kidding, honest! But, yeah, the Bennigans of Portage Country aren't exactly down on their luck these days. They didn't have an easy time of it, though, when they arrived from Scotland in the 1870s to help build the Kent railway."

"Hmm, I see."

Joel pulled up behind the minivan, put the Blazer in park, but left the engine and the air-conditioner running. He turned toward her. "Seriously, Val, we haven't talked much about my family. Just so you don't feel like you're walking into the middle of a movie, what can I tell you about the Bennigans?"

He's so kind. He wants to make this easier for me.

Val rubbed her left temple where a headache was being born, despite her pain-relief medication. She must be more anxious about this dinner than she'd realized. "Oh, a bit of family history, I guess. What they do for a living, where they got their money. Stuff like that. Family skeletons I should know about."

"OK, the abridged version, although I can't think of any skeletons," began Joel. "Three Bennigan brothers came to work on the railroad and stayed to hack a homestead out of the Ohio wilderness. They owned a good chunk of land back then—a couple of thousand acres—where they raised cattle, horses, and crops. They supplied oats to the Quaker Oats company in Akron—"

"Oh! That would explain that rather large collection

of Quaker Oats tins in your. . .eh, in our kitchen."

Joel broke into a grin, the laugh lines around his eyes spreading like the rays of the sun. "Right. Those tins have been in the family a long time, so don't drop any, or Millie will have a fit." He turned to regard Val fondly. "Anyway, around the turn of the century, the Bennigans opened the first dry-goods store in Kent. The enterprise was successful—so successful that they began concentrating on the grocery business rather than farming. In time, they sold off most of the land, but the dry-goods business prospered. These days, the Bennigan market chain stretches across Ohio."

"Uh huh. So, you'll never want for a job."

"You might say that, although I believe my calling is in the church rather than business. We've had quite a few ministers in the family over the years. Some politicians, too—local as well as a couple on the national level. Our family—and your family now, too—helped found Faith Bible over a hundred years ago."

"I'm impressed," said Val. "I did quite well for myself, didn't I?"

Joel put his hand over hers. It was an affectionate, reassuring gesture. "I think I'm the one who did well for myself, Val, on the day you agreed to marry me."

Val felt her throat tighten. She looked away, peering through the thin haze of heat at the sculpted bushes surrounding the house. She tried to focus on the gardening skills behind that sculpting rather than on the emotion behind Joel's words. Her own emotions were too fragile to hand him her heart just like that. He was so kind, so nice, such a romantic. But what if he was in love with the old Val, not the Val she was today? What if the new Val would end up driving him away?

What if she fell in love with him, then lost him?

She couldn't chance that. Such a loss would shatter what was left of her. . .completely. "I hope you don't live to regret that day," she said quietly, never taking her eyes off the bushes that seemed to shimmer in the humid heat.

fifteen

"Val, dear, welcome!"

Millie Bennigan wiped her hands on her apron and stretched out her freckled, plump arms. The kitchen was warm and fragrant with freshly baked cookies. There was a trace of laughter in Millie's voice. "My, my, my, it's a blessed day to have you back home!"

Val stepped into the short woman's embrace and allowed herself to be hugged. It felt good. Better, in fact, that she was willing to admit, even to herself. Like the "ahh" of weary limbs sinking into a dozen down comforters. After a few moments, Val pulled back. "Thank you, Millie. I'm glad to. . .be back."

"And you're lovelier than ever," Millie said, putting her hand against the side of Val's face. "Isn't she, Joel?"

Behind Val, Joel's voice boomed baritone in contrast to his mother's contralto. "You bet, Ma. My wife, the most beautiful woman in the world."

"Oh, Val, dear, how I cried when I saw how they'd cut off your pretty hair."

Val was surprised at the depth of the older woman's concern. "It's OK, Millie. It grew in thicker than I remember."

"You still remember only the time before you came to us, don't you?"

"Yes," said Val quietly.

"You were one of us, dear. A Bennigan by marriage. You're still one of us, whether or not you ever remember the past two years. Please God, there'll be many years of happy family memories to come. And don't the doctors say your memory might return?"

Val nodded. "Dr. Silverman says there's a chance." What she didn't say was that if two or three years passed with no memory recall, chances were those two years were lost forever. As it was, her own hopes grew slimmer with each passing day.

"Well, then," said Millie with an air of motherly authority as she untied her apron, "we'll just have to keep praying, won't we?"

"Thank you, Millie. You're a treasure."

"Oh, it takes one to know one," said Millie, shifting out of her sentimental mode and into her bustling mode. She pushed back a few stray gray hairs that escaped the bun at the back of her head. Her lined face creased into a smile, and the crow's feet around her faded denim eyes deepened. "Now, dears, come along and have a soft drink before dinner. Since this is your first day back, Val, I'll let you off spud-peeling duty."

Joel lifted the lid of a huge cast-iron pot that bubbled furiously on the gas range. "An idle threat, Ma. The spuds are done already."

"Just a figure of speech, son. A harmless figure of speech. Now, come along, you two." She put her hand under Val's elbow and steered her out of the sun-filled kitchen. "By the way, dear, nice dress. Very summery and pretty."

"Glad you like it," said Val, wondering silently if Millie had helped her buy it. Despite her mother-in-law's warm sincerity, Val's memory gaps made her feel on edge, out of kilter, slightly paranoid. Like when she was a kid, wondering what people knew about her secret family life. The can of worms behind closed doors. *What do the Bennigans know that I don't know? Even if I felt comfortable with them once, can I ever feel comfortable with them again?*

Joel bounded ahead to slide open the massive golden oak doors leading into the living room. The room was alive with laughter and chatter. Everywhere Val looked, children and adults lounged about, playing board games, visiting and talking, just like any other large family waiting for Sunday dinner.

The talking stopped when she stepped through the doorway. All eyes came to rest on her. Val swallowed hard. Her knees felt weak. She was on display again. Vulnerable. Exposed. Her nerves were taut, to the point that the soft strains of Mozart seemed to exacerbate her headache as much as the loudest, most discordant rap music. The pain-relief medication wasn't working. Or maybe her anxiety was working overtime. Val knew she was letting old mistrust take over, but her mouth felt dry and her pulse raced.

"Think positively, Val," her psychologist had said. "Take the initiative. People are going to be uncomfortable around you at first. Do something to put them at ease." She scanned the faces of eight adults and two children, and saw nothing but goodwill and openness. *OK, Dr. Ross. I can do this. It's only a Sunday dinner. No big thing.*

With a quick prayer, Val stepped into the cool green room and into her old reporter's persona. Working for the newspaper, she'd acquired the skill of acting confidently with an interviewee, even when her knees were practically knocking together. That professional mask had served her well during those years and had landed her many interviews that she'd crafted into newsworthy stories.

Maybe it could help her now.

She remembered Robert Bennigan best. A handsome man with salt-and-pepper hair and a heavy mustache, Mr. Bennigan had come to the hospital more often than the others. Today he was leaning against the white marble fireplace, puffing a sweet-smelling pipe. "Robert!" Val cried. "How nice to see you. Thank you for all your visits."

Val sensed that her smile looked fixed and uneasy, like a poorly constructed rubber mask. But she kept grinning at Robert anyway as she walked toward him. She was glad she'd left her walking cane behind in the Blazer. A cane spoke of weakness, and she wanted to appear strong. But when she spoke, her voice had the wooden quality of a voice thrown by a ventriloquist. Would she, could she, ever feel spontaneous with these people? Like she belonged?

If Robert thought her friendliness forced, he possessed the good grace not to show it. He lowered his pipe, deposited it on the mantel, and clasped Val's hand, pumping it. "Young lady, you're a sight for sore eyes. Welcome home! Here, have the seat of honor."

He ushered her to one of the hunter-green velvet Queen Anne armchairs beside the fireplace. She sat, perching uneasily on the edge of the overstuffed seat. Joel stood behind her, one hand on the wing of the chair as if they were posing for a photographic portrait—the ideal husband and wife. The rest of the family clustered around.

Val took her cue and turned reporter. "Since my memory of the past two years has been wiped out, 1 can't remember any of you, even though I wish I could," she said, slowly looking from face to face. "So let's start at the beginning. Let's pretend I'm a reporter for the *Kent-Ravenna Record Courier* and I'm doing a feature article on the Bennigans."

"Why would the newspaper want to write a story about us?" asked a small dark-haired boy whom Val guessed to be around eight or nine.

"Hush now, Petey," cooed Millie, tousling the boy's bushy hair. "This is a 'let's pretend' game."

"Exactly," said Val. "Let's pretend I need to gather enough information about each one of you so I can write a story to knock the socks off every newspaper reader in Kent."

"I like it," said Joel, looking pleased and proud.

"Great," said Val honestly, shooting Joel a smile. "Let's begin with you, Millie. Where did you come from originally? And how did you meet this devastatingly handsome husband of yours?"

~

An hour later when the family sat down to a dinner that rivaled a Thanksgiving feast, Val had a working knowledge of her in-laws. Dark-haired Matthew was Joel's only brother, married to Sarah. Petey and Andrew were their children, with another on the way. Charity, the oldest sister, was Val's age. She'd just completed her degree in social work. In her spare time, she taught handicapped children to ride horses.

The two other sisters, identical twins with long, tawny hair the color of Joel's, were Faith and Hope, thus completing Millie's in-house circle of Christian virtues. The twins were undergraduates at KSU, both majoring in accounting and planning to go into the family business.

Ruthie, the severely retarded foster child, was sleeping upstairs.

"Poor dear, she's not having a good day," said Millie as she ladled the steaming corn chowder into country crock blue bowls.

"Is she difficult to care for?" asked Val, reaching for a warm, whole-wheat dinner roll. She couldn't imagine dealing with a retarded child.

"Well. . .yes and no," said Millie. "Of course, there are some medical procedures we've had to learn, but they're not difficult once you get the hang of catheters and handling seizures and so on. Ruthie was born profoundly physically and mentally handicapped. It was all too much for her young parents, so they put her in an institution."

"I see." Val buttered her bread. It smelled marvelous, hot and yeasty.

"We used to visit the home because of Charity's horseback-riding program for the better-functioning children—"

Val lifted one eyebrow. "Horseback riding?"

"You'd be amazed what good therapy it is!" Charity piped up, her dark eyes sparkling with enthusiasm. "Gives the kids a totally new outlook on themselves and their abilities—and it's lots of fun."

Val nodded, impressed with the young woman's dedication.

Millie passed a steaming bowl of soup to Val. She continued talking, the corners of her mouth turning downward pensively. "We used to visit the home and read Bible stories to the children, even to the severely disabled ones. Some people would say they're vegetables, but we don't agree. Many of these kids respond to love better than so-called normal people. Anyway, we grew terribly fond of Ruthie, didn't we, Robert? She can't talk but she'd always have that big, open-mouthed smile when she saw us. . ."

Millie looked at her husband who sat at the far end of the oblong table. He nodded in agreement, but Val noticed only the look of tenderness that flashed between them. Their love was so obvious, so rock-solid. She pretended to be absorbed in buttering another roll. The question that screamed inside her was one she didn't dare ask. Had she and Joel shared this kind of poignant intimacy? Had they exchanged looks such as this?

She glanced up from her buttering and caught Joel studying her. Across the white linen tablecloth and solid silver saltshakers, she saw something in his eyes that sent unsettling but velvet quivers down her spine. It was as if he had heard her unspoken question. Suddenly, the air seemed thick. They were the only ones in the room. The intensity that darkened his blue eyes told her that yes, they'd looked at each other that way.

He's looking at me like that now! His eyes were drawing her into a deep well of emotion. If she didn't pull back, she'd drown.

Flustered, Val broke contact with Joel and dragged her attention back to Millie. "What then?" she prompted.

Millie cleared her throat. "We couldn't bear to leave her there, in the institution. It was a good facility, the best. But the girl needed the love of a family. We applied for adoption, but the authorities would only allow us to be foster parents. We've had her for six years now."

"Did. . .did I know Ruthie? Before?"

Millie looked at Val with great compassion. "Yes,

dear. From the beginning, you were very fond of our Ruthie. Many a time, you'd sit with her, reading her the papers you wrote for your classes. She loved that. She'd laugh and laugh, rocking back and forth in her wheel-chair until we were afraid she'd loosen her restraining devices and fall out. She'd laugh even when the subject wasn't remotely funny."

Val smiled. "So she liked the attention?"

"Oh, my, yes. It was always very heartwarming to see you two together. And although she can't talk, I believe she's missed you terribly these past six months." Millie stood and pushed her chair back. "Robert, dear, would you mind carving the roast? I need to see if the Yorkshire pudding is finished."

"Yorkshire pudding?" asked Val. "The British contri-bution to roast beef dinners?"

Millie hurried toward the kitchen, talking as she went, "Yes, I made it for you, Val, dear. You were fond of it when you came back from Ireland."

Val sent a questioning glance in Joel's direction. "Did my trip to Ireland have something to do with my inves-tigation of the cult?"

He nodded and helped himself to some more golden chowder from the blue ceramic tureen. "Right. I went after you and somehow managed to persuade you to come home. Not long after that, we were married."

Val blinked. She'd absorbed so much information in the last few hours, her head felt heavy. She savored another spoonful of Millie's corn chowder. The woman was a wizard in the kitchen, Val realized. Suddenly, she felt ashamed of her own pathetic cooking skills. *Poor Joel, he gave up all this for burned macaroni and cheese?*

Charity was just asking Val to pass the salt when a bone-chilling scream came from upstairs, splitting the tranquil afternoon. Robert jumped up, knocking his chair over. "Ruthie! She's had another nightmare. I'll handle it."

The scream built to a high-pitched howl.

Millie shot out of the kitchen, wiping her hands on a dishcloth, and both husband and wife rushed up the main staircase off the foyer. To Val's ears, the screams sounded maniacal. Shaken, she panned the faces around the table. The family seemed concerned, but not frantic.

"It's OK, Val," said Charity, who was sitting beside Val. "Ruthie often wakes up with nightmares. She'll be all right in a minute, just as soon as she realizes where she is."

Val nodded, staring at the doorway through which Millie and Robert had disappeared. Overhead, she heard footsteps, followed by diminished wailing.

After a few more minutes, the shrieks gave way to loud sobbing. The funereal stillness around the table was broken only by the chink of ice as Joel drank from his glass.

The screaming spooked Val. The corn chowder, so sweet and creamy a moment ago, suddenly turned gritty in her mouth. "Does she. . .have many of these nightmares?" she asked no one in particular.

"They've increased over the past year or so," said Joel. "The doctors aren't sure why. Maybe some chemical malfunction in the brain."

"Isn't there any way to stop them?" Val asked, wide-eyed, her spoon in midair.

"Her new medication helps some," Joel replied. "We give her lots of extra attention. And we pray with her before she falls asleep. But other than that, there doesn't seem to be a cure for whatever is bothering her."

Val's eyes narrowed. "So you just live with it?"

"I guess that's about the size of it." He shrugged. "She's part of our family. Her problems are our problems. We let her know she's loved and just muddle through."

Val started to speak, but faltered. This love for Ruthie, a damaged girl doomed to life in an institution, was sticking in her throat like dry bread. She lowered her eyes, unwilling to show how shaken she was. Shaken by the animal terror of the child's wailing, then by her own trembling amazement at the Bennigans' capacity for love. She stirred her spoon aimlessly in her soup as her appetite evaporated.

Joel reached for more iced tea. "Anyway, a great French writer once defined a Christian as someone to whom God has entrusted the care of his creation. We try to take care of Ruthie as best we can. She can't help it. . . being the way she is."

His words struck Val like a brick to the head. *She can't help it. But they love her anyway.*

Silence crept into the dining room and pulled up a seat at the table. The only sounds in the high-ceilinged room were the clinking of soup spoons against china and the rattling of ice cubes. Now and then, the adults glanced uneasily at each other. Even the children fell quiet. The silence didn't dissipate until Robert appeared in the doorway pushing a wheelchair. Millie followed closely.

When Val saw the gnarled scrap of humanity imprisoned in the mechanized wheelchair, she flinched. The girl's crooked limbs were folded in upon her wizened body. Her head, held upright by a neck brace attached to the wheelchair, was tilted back so that she was staring at the ceiling, her mouth open as wide as a beached fish. She was groaning.

Oh, Lord! So much suffering!

Charity touched Val's forearm, but Val hardly registered the gesture. The skin on the back of her neck twitched. How should she handle this? She'd known this child once. How should she renew their friendship? Should she take the initiative again?

Val rose to her feet and moved across the room, toward the wheelchair. "Hi, there!" she said with forced enthusiasm. "Ruthie, guess who's back?"

At the sound of her name, the girl transferred her gaze from the ceiling to the source of the voice. Her hollow, dark eyes blinked, stared, widened. Her groaning accelerated into grunts. Her breathing became labored.

"Ruthie! It's Val. Remember me?" Val held out her hand.

This time, taking the initiative had been a mistake.

A big one.

Ruthie squirmed, struggled, and fought as she tried to distance herself from Val. She shrieked as if Val were coming at her with hot pokers or electrical prods. Wrenching her head from side to side, the girl flopped her withered arms, as pathetic as a penguin trying to fly. Her elfin legs strained against the restraining straps.

But the screams! They stopped Val cold, causing her adrenaline to pump as if ten fire alarms had gone off at once. The child was terrified of her! Stunned, Val backed up against the wall. She fought against being sucked into Ruthie's vortex of fear. Why was the girl afraid? Did she think Val had returned from the dead?

What? Val labored to breathe.

"Val—"

She heard Joel's voice behind her, but it was drowned out by Ruthie's screams. Then the screaming spiraled into shrill wailing. Suddenly, Ruthie's face began twitching violently. Her head jerked back and forth like a broken doll being shaken by an angry child.

With Val looking on, the girl's mangled body convulsed. Her eyes rolled back. She bit her lip, and bloody foam dribbled down her chin.

A seizure! Oh, dear God, I've caused her to have a seizure!

Robert held Ruthie's head steady while Millie barked orders. "Charity, get me that soft cushion on the couch for her head. Joel, time the seizure. Faith, bring a wet washcloth."

As if from far away, Val heard a small boy sobbing and his mother comforting him. Val stood mesmerized as the others swarmed around the wheelchair. They worked together like a well-oiled engine. But something other than shock was holding Val in its icy grip. A memory. A memory that was rattling around in her brain, but kept eluding her. This scene, this ugliness, ignited neural pathways she'd traveled before.

Recently.

Val bit her knuckle. The memory was banging on the door, demanding admittance. Filled with suspicion, then dread, Val thought she recognized the knock. She tried to ignore it, deny it. Meanwhile, before her eyes, Ruthie thrashed like some small animal caught in a trap. Val could pinpoint the moment the girl lost consciousness.

The seizure was a grand mal.

Then memory kicked down the door.

Val saw not Ruthie's poor body in spasms—but her own. Val had suffered a seizure in the hospital, several times. She must have looked just as hideous and spastic, losing her dignity and self-control. Even now the doctors kept her on anti-seizure medication. Perhaps she'd need it for the rest of her life.

Like Ruthie, she was damaged. Crippled. Because of her brain injury, it was possible that the electrical impulses in her brain could run amuck at any time, with or without warning. Anytime, anyplace, with anyone, she could fall to the floor, a writhing, grotesque, almost inhuman. . .thing.

Suddenly, Val's thoughts took on a cold, moon-far quality about them, as if they were coming not from her, but from some ghostly visitant sitting on her shoulder, exhaling its foul breath of fear down her neck. *Run! Escape your fate! You're every bit as maimed as this girl!*

Shock became anxiety and anxiety, grief. Val was sure that everyone in the room knew that she could have a seizure just like Ruthie. Her exposure felt as complete and as painful as if the flesh had been stripped from her bones. A scream caught at the back of her throat. Quaking, tears streaming down her face, she bolted from the dining room, through the foyer, and wrenched open the double front doors.

Weeping, she fled into a breezeless heat so oppressive, so leaden, that it seemed bent on squeezing the life out of her.

sixteen

Val ran into the sweltering afternoon, not knowing where she was going and not caring. Ashamed and confused by her panicky reaction, she lurched past the flowerbed overflowing with blue delphiniums and past the sculpted bushes. Following the gravel driveway that led into the four-car garage out back, she skirted the trees laden with small green apples, then darted across the open area behind the house, past the out buildings, heading toward the woods that shimmered mistily in the heat.

She wasn't sure what horror she was trying to escape, but she ran as if her life depended on it. Shaking like a leaf in a storm, her weak leg gave out several times. Twice she fell. Both times, she clambered to her feet and ran on recklessly.

Streaks of dirt and grass stained her blue and white dress, and bits of dried weeds clung to her white pumps. Her right leg hurt, but she kept running. Reaching the woods at last, she stumbled into the eerie stillness beneath the trees.

She leaned against a thick old trunk, gasping for breath, gulping the humid air. Her heart was pounding wildly; her knees, ready to buckle beneath her. Her whole body felt rubbery and unreal. The heat had silenced the birds, but overhead, two vultures circled and screeched. *There must be something dead in the woods.*

Seized with dread, she backed out, then fled along the

edge of the dark green depths in which small animals huddled, hiding from the sun. The foliage curled and sagged as if in heat prostration. Twigs snapped underfoot. Brambles snagged her dress, ripping it. She could no longer see the house, and she hoped no one could see her. What would they think of her, bolting like a wild thing?

But she couldn't stay and witness her future. . .if such horror *were* her future.

Her stomach churned. Nausea. Was it the heat? Or was the bile of fear poisoning her?

A stitch in her side sent shooting pains through her torso as she rounded the evergreens at the end of the wood. There, an unexpected sight greeted her, ending her flight. Before her stretched a large manmade lake, easily the size of a football field. The magnificent span of water lazily mirrored the cloudless sky of liquid sapphire.

"Oh!" she caught her breath.

The sight jolted her like something jumping out of the shadows. But once she'd stopped, whatever was pursuing her overtook her. Dizzy with sensations of disorientation she'd never experienced before, she covered her face with her hands and sank to the ground near a cluster of birches. Dry grass and pine needles pricked her knees, ripping her hose, but she didn't notice.

She was completely unprepared for the raging, full-blown panic attack that slammed into her. Her breath caught in her throat. A sense of catastrophe suffused her, smothering her. She'd read about these attacks, but she'd never experienced one before. Dr. Ross had warned her about them, even telling her what to expect should she suddenly find the earth opening up to swallow her.

In the safety of Dr. Ross's office, Val had thought that anxiety attacks could never happen to her. Now she was in the grip of one, perhaps triggered by the stress of coming home or the horror of causing and witnessing Ruthie's seizure. The panic was a savage thing—much worse than the textbook descriptions.

It winded her. Breathing was reduced to wheezing.

Despite the hot July day, Val felt chilled. She was falling, falling, falling into a frigid bottomless abyss filled with dead stars. Her stomach churned with the sensation. The plummeting was so real—like a roller-coaster drop of a free-falling elevator—it sent her heart racing, pounding. She closed her eyes, as if that might break her fall.

Cold sweat beaded on her face and trickled down her back. She rocked back and forth, seeking in infantile movement the comfort of everyday sanity that had disappeared into the cracked earth. Blood thundered in her ears.

She curled her fists into her hair and tried to stop the shaking, to steady herself. Struggling to breathe against the tremendous weight pressing into her chest, she gulped in air, never getting enough.

Was she dying? Or just losing her mind?

"Val! Val! Are you all right?"

Joel's worried voice broke through her quaking.

He knelt beside her and took her hands, bringing them to his face. "Your hands are freezing."

She looked at him, studying his features, at first not registering who he was.

"Val, what's the matter?" His voice was soothing. "You're so pale."

Suddenly, as if scales fell from her eyes, she saw him.

His face, the way he was looking at her, so worried, so concerned, so. . .full of love. His sky-blue eyes were solemn and tender, his love, anchoring her in the reality of the moment. She held his hands, digging her nails into his flesh, laboring to breathe in more than shallow scoops. With each ragged breath, she tried to gather the threads of her unraveled nerves and wind them back into a tight ball.

"It's an anxiety attack, isn't it?" he asked, wiping her tears with the pads of his thumbs.

She nodded, not trusting her voice.

Gently, he placed his hands on her shoulders and squeezed. "It's OK, Val. Everything's OK now. You're safe. I won't let anything hurt you."

He drew her to himself. Her body went limp. His hands splayed across her damp shoulder blades, molding her to his chest. She felt his heart beating, strong and steady. She closed her eyes and found she could breathe normally. Safely. His muscled arms tightened around her. The anxiety ebbed, as if a wound had been lanced, leaving her spent and exhausted.

Above them, a dry breeze crept through the wilted leaves.

The wind—she didn't know where it came from or where it was going. The wind—free-wheeling as an anxiety attack, always skulking in the bushes, ready to blow her away. She could no more stop or control a panic attack than she could stop the wind.

"Val, let's go home. We'll call Dr. Ross."

Val cleared her throat. "What about. . .the family, dinner?" Even to herself, her voice sounded creaky as an old garden gate hinge.

"You can sit in the Blazer, and I'll go in and tell them

you're not feeling well. You don't have to face them again until you feel better. Maybe today was an overload, with Ruthie and all."

"Ruthie? Is she. . .OK?"

He nodded. "Seeing you was just too big a shock. But she's calm now."

Val rubbed her eyes. The panic had subsided. "Should I go see her?"

"Not yet. Let's give her more time to get used to the idea of your return. She'll be fine. Now, let's go home."

"All right," she said, too weak to protest.

He took her face between his hands. His eyes were blue gaslight flames. "I won't let anything hurt you, ever," he whispered, his voice raw.

The wind disturbed the foliage again, moaning through the tops of the towering conifers. It sounded small and baleful. Although the day was almost blinding in its brightness, Val found the inevitability of the wind dark and ominous.

Val looked deeply into Joel's eyes. She felt she was touching his soul. How could she tell him the truth without hurting him? Especially when he looked at her like that. She shook her head. "Joel, Joel, Joel, that's a promise you can't keep."

He pulled back, stunned. Then understanding crept across his features. His hands dropped to her shoulders, then to her upper arms. The downward motion seemed an admission of defeat. "I suppose you're right."

Val stared up at the sky. Cold blue. Infinitely so, maybe. As a child, she'd thought that heaven was up in the blue yonder. Heaven. She still remembered the disappointment of being sent back from heaven. After her accident, she'd seen the life beyond, touched it even, but she'd been turned away and had fallen back to earth.

She met Joel's gaze again. "We don't control anything," she stated, hearing the quiver in her voice. "Our lives can change in an instant. You can't protect me from hurt, or panic attacks, or seizures, or car accidents, even though you want to."

Joel's look disturbed her. "You're right. I can't protect you from everything. But I promised to love and cherish you in sickness and in health, in good times and in bad. What I can do is keep my promises."

She looked at him with compassion. He meant those words, he really did.

But when the winds blew and became a tornado and tore through their house, imploding the windows, ripping off the roof, and destroying all in its path—what, then?

seventeen

Summer finally burned itself out. The blazing heat died down to flickering embers and began mellowing into the orange-gold of autumn. Val had been home six weeks, and her life was falling apart. More often than not, she cried herself to sleep. She still slept alone. Her memory had not returned, and the multiple stresses of therapy, of readjusting to life outside the hospital, and of Joel's protectiveness and his toughness about enforcing her medical regimen were all taking their toll.

Although panic never attacked again with the soul-shattering brutality of that Sunday in the Bennigans' woods, Val felt disoriented much of the time, as if she were trying to navigate her way around an alien planet. Trying to master the everyday tasks of living—shopping for food, cooking, cleaning, using money, getting around town—overwhelmed her. Disheartened at the slowness of her progress, she shuffled through each day. The occupational therapist who made home visits was kind, but Val dreaded seeing her Volvo pull into the driveway.

Then there was physical therapy, the tedious business of strengthening her weak leg and improving her balance and endurance. Three times a week, Joel packed her into the Blazer and drove her to the clinic. On days when she balked, he bullied her into going. "You've got to do it, Val," he'd say. "You've got no choice."

At those times, she disliked Joel and was glad they didn't share a bedroom. Physical therapy tried her nerves as well as her muscles. She wanted to be better *now*. She'd been in therapy so long. The trek back to normalcy was taking so terribly long, like one of those forced marches imposed on prisoners during World War II.

Her own forgetfulness constantly tripped her up. Trying to find where she'd left the scissors could trigger an extended crying jag, along with many banged cupboard doors and slammed drawers. She burned pots and pans on a daily basis. The electric kettle was shot because she'd let it boil dry. In rehab, she'd been taught to use a day planner to keep track of tasks—from brushing her teeth to keeping appointments with her counselor. But even with this aid, she still forgot. Sometimes she even forgot what day it was and had to consult the calendar.

At times, life seemed just too, too hard.

And she seemed so useless, so unable to cope.

Then there was the question of whether she'd ever work again. All her life—all that she could remember of it, anyway—she'd earned her own money and paid her own way. Now she couldn't work or even go to school to prepare for work. She was totally dependent on Joel. And she was little or no help to him. Many days, he came home from work and had to cook dinner or order in pizza. He never complained, but Val wouldn't have blamed him if he considered her an insufferable burden.

She kept praying for the return of her memory. If she could recall her earlier marriage to Joel, maybe things wouldn't be so hard. Maybe she'd connect with him again and stop resenting him. But she couldn't remember. With each day that passed, her fear grew stronger and her faith, weaker. At times, her confidence in the goodness of God seemed to be ebbing like the tide. Why wasn't God answering? Why didn't He restore her lost years? Was she driving Him away, too?

Everything about her life—the days filled with therapy, conflicts, difficulties, and bad cooking—made her angry. And she took that anger out on Joel.

Her uneasy temper dismayed her. At the slightest provocation, her anger could flare out of control like a flame leaping from a burning skillet and spreading across a grease-spattered stove top. A dirty milk glass Joel left in the kitchen sink was enough to set her off. "Joel Bennigan," she scolded, "do you think I'm your scullery maid, good for nothing else but cleaning up your sticky messes?" But if she made Joel's life miserable, it was because she was miserable herself.

After each outburst, she'd chastise herself bitterly and resolve to count to ten the next time. But when the next time came, it was the same old story. If her weekly session with Dr. Ross about controlling these outbursts was having any effect, she couldn't see it. "Lack of impulse control," he'd called it. Day by day, she grew more cantankerous and drove Joel farther away. She hated herself for doing it, but she couldn't seem to stop acting like a shrew.

Then, sometime in September, as the summer lay dying, she decided that Joel would be better off without her. But not without making one last valiant effort.

※

She'd spent all afternoon trying to bake peanut butter cookies. Joel liked them. She'd asked him before he left for his office at the church that morning. Val was in a rare good mood and wanted to do something nice to surprise her husband when he got home, a small peace offering, a wifely gesture of affection. To have him return to the aroma of baking cookies would seem homey, something like walking into the comfort of Millie's kitchen.

She wanted to make a home for him, a real home—not some modified rehab center with her as the patient and him as the caretaker.

But the baking wasn't going well. With the first batch, she'd set the oven too high and had forgotten to grease the cookie sheet. The charred cookie remains clung pitifully to the aluminum. The next dozen went in at the correct temperature, but Val had misplaced the timer and couldn't figure out how to use the electrical one wired into the stove. Since she hadn't checked the clock when she put the dough in, she had to guesstimate. Her timing was off and cookies were burned around the edges, though more presentable than the first batch.

Determined to make the best of things, she scraped the most edible cookies off the sheet with a plastic spatula and arranged them on an oversized ceramic plate she'd found in the dining room hutch. The plate had Navajo designs and highly fired glossy colors. It was an expensive, handmade piece of pottery, most likely a wedding gift, since Joel had never mentioned that they'd taken a vacation to the Southwest.

The small mountain of cookies, like so many brown pebbles with dark crispy edges, looked attractive enough set against the vivid russet and turquoise of the plate. Proudly, she placed her triumph on the kitchen table where Joel could see it as soon as he walked into the room. Encouraged by this small victory, Val decided that she'd make a meal that didn't come from a can or the supermarket freezer. Joel had eaten far too many Hungry Man frozen TV dinners.

Break down a task into manageable steps. After consulting the cookbooks, she decided that a reasonably easy meal would be western omelettes. She checked to see that there were green peppers, onions, tomatoes, cheddar cheese, and eggs in the fridge. Then she broke the project into steps—beginning with assembling the ingredients—and wrote each step on a three-by-five card.

Seeing an overview of the entire job boosted her confidence. To celebrate her buoyant mood, she slipped a Michael Card CD into the stereo and hummed along with his songs of praise while she chopped and cut. Finally, saucers of chopped green pepper, diced onions, sliced tomatoes, shredded cheese, plus a bowl of canary-colored beaten eggs lined the counter. Everything was ready to be assembled and cooked.

Val checked the kitchen clock. Five P.M. Joel was usually home by 5:30. By counting backwards, she figured she'd have enough time to set the dining room table with the good china and the yellow linen tablecloth, light a couple of candles, mix some iced tea, change into her good black pants, and put the eggs on to cook at 5:20. Everything would be ready just as Joel walked in the door.

Won't he be surprised?

She followed her plan to the minute, taking several seconds out to admire the table. Everything glimmered and gleamed in the flickering candlelight. Tonight would be a far cry from burned macaroni and cheese. Maybe she was making progress, after all. If she could handle meal prep, maybe it wasn't too soon to dream about going back to KSU and getting on with her degree.

ஐ

Val glanced at the clock again.

At 6:05 P.M., two golden omelettes bursting with cheese and vegetables sat on the serving platter on the counter. At 5:30, they'd been piping hot, but their sizzle was long gone.

Where are you, Joel Bennigan?

She leaned against the butcher-block island in the middle of the kitchen, crossed her arms, and stared at her ruined dinner. *How could he do this to me? Tonight of all nights?* Her jaw clenched and her foot tapped as her anger simmered. Maybe he had a reasonable excuse. Maybe he'd run out of gas.

Not likely, though. Mechanically-minded Joel always kept the gas tank at least half full.

At 6:13, he sauntered through the front door.

This better be good, mister.

She didn't go out to meet him. Instead, she listened and fumed as his footsteps echoed down the hallway. He stopped to hang up his jacket in the closet. She heard the closet door slide shut. Her foot continued to tap.

"Hi, Val! I'm home. Sorry I'm late. There was an emergency at church—" Joel stopped dead and surveyed the scene before him: one boiling hot wife and two cold omelettes. "Uh, I guess I should have called first." Grimacing, he glanced down at the bucket of Kentucky Fried Chicken in his hands.

"You might have told me if my cooking wasn't good enough!"

She knew she was being unreasonable. But her eighteen-wheeler had just blown a tire and the brakes had failed and she was careening down the highway at suicidal speed. Not only that, but the contents of that truck were about to be violently disgorged.

Joel's gaze settled on the plate of cookies on the table. His face fell. For a moment, he looked as crestfallen as a small boy who'd just broken his mother's favorite vase.

He glanced across the room at Val, his blue eyes wide. "Val, I'm sorry to disappoint you and ruin your plans, I really am. I know you're annoyed, but please calm down. For your own sake, if not for mine."

Wrong! The wrong thing to say. But anything he said at that moment would have been wrong. "Don't you patronize me, Joel Bennigan! You think you can just waltz in here any old time and expect your little brain-damaged wife to keep her cool—"

"Val! Stop doing this to yourself. . .to us!"

She felt her face heat. "Don't tell me what to do! I'm sick of you telling me what to do and what not to do. Do you hear me? Sick to death!"

Joel looked at her in dismay. "What are you talking about?"

"What am I talking about? You can't be serious, Mr. Gestapo! Every time I turn around, it's 'Val, have you taken your medication?' 'Val, have you done your physical therapy exercises?' 'Val, did you fill in your date book?' Listen here, mister, I've about had it with your control—"

His brows furrowed deeply. Edginess entered his voice. "My. . .*control?*"

"Your running, managing my life! I'm not a child! And contrary to popular opinion, I'm *not* disabled!" She was shouting now. "You're not my caretaker! Not my warden, nor my coach!"

"Val—"

"You're so mean. . .I hate you!"

She stood in the middle of the kitchen, the island separating them, with her fists balled at her sides and her shoulders rigid. She was still shouting. "Do you know what it's like not to be able to remember? To have to relearn how to take a shower? How to write a check? To cook the simplest meal? To send a retarded girl into a seizure? Let me tell you—it makes me feel like a *freak!*"

With that, she exploded. All the hurt and anger and rage that had accumulated since the accident burst out, like the ocean crashing through a dam. With one jerk of her arm, Val sent the clutter on the island clattering to the floor: the fruit basket, the mail, a mug of pens and pencils, her date book, a glass of iced tea.

She threw open cupboards, grabbing random items—glasses, plates, jars, canned goods—and flinging them across the room in Joel's general direction. He jumped backward, dropping the bucket of chicken and flinging up his arms to protect his head.

"Stop it, Val! Don't be crazy!"

Val slammed a cupboard door so hard the top hinge broke and the door flapped crookedly. Slam! Slam! Slam! More cupboard doors. Crash! The skillet hit the floor. Crack! The drawer of silverware clattered across the linoleum.

Joel moved toward her, one hand sheltering his head, the other outstretched. "Honey, calm down. I know you're mad, but this isn't solving anything—"

"Mad? You haven't begun to see mad!"

She dodged around the island, avoiding him. "Leave me alone! Don't you get it? Stop running my life. Stop bullying me into therapy. Stop checking up on me. *Leave me alone!*"

Joel stopped in his tracks. The rage unfolding before his eyes startled him. He'd no idea it had been building up. Sure, he'd known Val was under tremendous stress, but he hadn't suspected this boiling cauldron. He stood stunned as Val grabbed the plate of cookies off the kitchen table and barreled toward the door.

"Val, wait—"

"I baked these for you—take them!" she yelled.

"What?"

The full meaning of her words didn't register, even when she swirled around and hurled the plate at him. Airborne cookies scattered like hailstones while Val dashed from the kitchen, down the hallway, out the front door, not waiting to see if her projectile had hit its mark.

Joel froze, registering danger, but unable to move. There was a shower of cookies in slow motion. The heavy plate sailed through the air like a graceful turquoise and russet bird. Things didn't speed up until the ceramic plate—a wedding gift from his brother Matthew who had a fondness for all things Native American—broadsided him on the left temple.

Blood spurting, Joel crashed to the floor like a felled buffalo.

eighteen

Ten minutes later, Val was walking aimlessly along the streets of Kent, heading into the beginnings of a late summer sunset. Sheaves of pale pink were spreading through the sky, staining the horizon with hints of more vivid hues. But Val didn't notice the beauty of the fading day. The intensity of her anger had scraped her nerves raw, and now the fury had spent itself, leaving her depressed, ashamed, and exhausted.

She was surprised when she ended up at the university. She flopped onto a wooden bench beside a flowerbed filled with orange mums. Burying her face in her hands, she struggled to regain control of her emotions. What had she said in the white madness of anger? What had she done? Wrecked her kitchen, broken a cupboard door, thrown a plate of cookies at Joel. . . .

Surely, it hadn't hit him. She didn't remember taking time to aim properly. She'd just flung it toward him. Why? A stupid parting gesture, like getting in the last word. The heavy Navajo plate couldn't have struck him. . .could it? He'd have seen it coming and stepped out of the way, wouldn't he?

Val pushed back her hair and tried to think clearly. Three students walked by, laden with heavy backpacks, and stared at her. Did she look that distraught? The students moved on and Val shook her head, as if arguing with herself. She couldn't believe that she would physically hurt her husband. Such a thing just couldn't happen.

She got to her feet and started walking again. At least her right leg was stronger these days. Maybe more walking would clear her mind. She trekked over the grassy commons, up and down the wooded hills, around the gym where the infamous student shootings had taken place on May 4, 1970.

Val was fighting her own war. An inner battle. "Look to the roots of your anger," Dr. Ross had said. "Try to see what's going on beyond the surface stuff that's irritating you."

Val was aware that there was more to her anger than a husband who had come home late for his dinner. But nothing she'd said had made sense to Joel, she was sure of that. She'd barely made sense to herself. Val stopped at a water fountain and rubbed her temples, suddenly realizing she had a ferocious tension headache. Since the accident, she'd almost gotten used to them.

The water was cold and good. She drank, then stood and watched the sunset. Did she really believe that her words and accusations had made no sense? Or had she spoken the truth in anger, no matter how garbled? That she was sick and tired of Joel as her guardian?

That was a hard thing to admit in the cool moments of sanity. After all Joel had done for her. . .standing by her when she didn't even remember who he was. Still the faithful husband, caring for her, supporting her. . .and yet. . .she needed him to back off. Like she'd said, she wasn't a child. Her demands sounded so ungrateful, and yet. . . .

The setting sun finally got down to serious business as she left the campus and walked down Main Street. Pinks and mauves shimmied across the western sky like the unfurling of a silk scarf. After some deliberation,

Val decided to drop by Faith Bible's sanctuary. She needed to think, to pray. A big decision needed to be made—and she couldn't wait much longer. . . .

๛

Joel opened his eyes. His head ached—fiercely. Dazed, he sat up. Pieces of broken pottery lay scattered on the floor. The smell of blood mingled with the smell of singed peanut butter cookies and the fainter aroma of fried chicken. He put his hand to his throbbing head. It came away bloody.

Knees wobbly, Joel struggled to his feet. He grabbed a clean dish towel from a drawer by the sink. With each step, he ground cookie crumbs into the floor. Cringing at the shooting pain, he pressed the towel to his head to absorb the blood and staunch the flow. Then, gingerly he felt around the wound.

Luckily, it wasn't much more than a scrape. He'd suffered worse during a dozen football skirmishes. Maybe he'd have someone take a look at it later, but right now he had more important business.

"Val?"

The only sound in the house was the heavy ticking of the grandfather clock.

"Val, are you here?"

Pressing harder on the towel, Joel hurried to the open front door. He pushed the screen door and it swung outward with the tired exhalation of a worn tension spring. He stepped out onto the porch, hoping to find Val perched on the steps or sitting on the bench under the cherry tree.

No sign of her.

He checked the street in both directions.

It was empty. The sky was smudged with crimson as the sun dipped behind the horizon. The humidity was waning. Darkness was coming on. Where could she have gone?

Back inside the house, Joel spotted Val's purse on the hall table. Wherever she'd gone, she had no money or identification with her. Still holding the side of his head, he loped upstairs. Maybe she was in the office or her bedroom. He raced from room to room. The emptiness seemed to mock him.

He checked his pockets for his keys and bounded down the stairs, unconcerned about his throbbing head. But halfway down the steps, he felt the tug of inspiration. He doubled back to his room and rummaged in the nightstand drawer until he found the item he'd suddenly remembered. Tucking it in inside his shirt, under the waistband of his jeans, he took the steps by twos and threes. Val might see meaning in this item. If he found her.

Still pressing the towel to his head, Joel tore off in the Blazer. He didn't know where to begin looking, and he didn't know what to think. Val had fled the house in such a emotional uproar. . .she wouldn't do anything stupid, would she? Like stepping off the curb in front of a car? Or jumping off the bridge into the river? He wondered if anything could surprise him on this strange evening. What if. . . .

Joel drove slowly along Main Street, then Water Street, scanning each sidewalk. A few students and shoppers were still straggling home, but no Val. She'd been wearing black pants and a bright green cotton sweater, a short-sleeved one. Where would she go? With no money, she'd hardly be in Brady's Coffee Shop or any of the fast-food joints that lined the strip leading to the university. He circled down around the bridge, just in case, then looked along the old railway tracks.

More frantic with every passing minute, Joel broke the speed limit to reach the campus. It was a pretty campus, lots of grassy areas, trees, flowers, a peaceful place for a walk. He and Val used to stroll here often in their previous life together. Yeah, the campus was his best bet, he decided. Abandoning the Blazer in a visitors' lot, he took off on foot.

He knew the walking paths well. Jogging, he covered them all in less than forty-five minutes. Still no sign of her. A couple of times, he bumped into people he knew and asked them if they'd seen his wife. With each shake of the head, his heart sank lower.

Finally, Joel collapsed on a bench and stared up at the black sky and the few early stars. The unseeing stars had no more knowledge of Val's whereabouts than he had.

But Someone did. *Why didn't I think of that before? I'll ask the One who knows all our comings and goings, our going out and our coming in, every move before we make it.* Joel shot to his feet and sprinted the few hundred yards to Faith Bible.

nineteen

There were no lights in the sanctuary. The only illumination came from streetlamps filtering through the stained-glass windows depicting gospel scenes. But in the dusk, all the colors were gray and shades of gray. Val sat in the front pew, hunched forward, head in hands, her mood reflecting her surroundings. When she heard someone slip in by the side door, she figured it was Mack. Not many people knew the side door was open until nine.

When Joel stood in front of her, holding what looked like a bloody dish towel to the side of his head, she started as if he were an apparition. As if by thinking so long, so hard, and so painfully about him, she'd conjured him up in some kind of waking dream.

But like Mary Magdalene on Easter morning, when she heard him call her name, she knew he was real.

"Val."

Alarmed, she jumped to her feet. "Your head!"

"Just a scratch."

"Did I. . .?" She couldn't bear to say the words.

Joel grinned easily. "Let's put it this way—you've got a great pitching arm."

"Joel! Don't joke about this! You're injured!"

"I've had worse. It's not fatal. Certainly nothing to match the bashing your head got. Don't worry, I'll live."

"Don't worry?" Val's voice rose. "Let me see."

Joel held the towel away from his head. Val stood on

159

tiptoe, clutching the pew, and leaned closer to him. "Here, turn toward me. Oh, I can't see. It's too dark in here."

"It's only a surface wound. A scratch."

"Do you need stitches?"

Joel felt the cut above his left ear. "Naw, I wouldn't say so. Feels like a small nick. Maybe half an inch, if that, above the hairline. Anyway, I'm an exjock, remember?"

Val frowned. "And what does that mean?"

"Jocks pride themselves on toughing it out. No running to the doc for scratches. Old habits die hard." He chuckled softly, then sobered."Are your headaches like this? Like a mad elephant just hauled off and kicked you in the side of the head?"

Val shrugged. "Something like that."

"I can tell you this," Joel said, checking the towel for fresh blood. "I certainly have a healthy chunk of empathy for you now. Hey, bleeding's stopped. No more worrying, OK?"

Val looked down at her hands. She was gripping the pew so tightly, her knuckles looked pale. "Joel. . .I'm so sorry. . .I didn't mean. . . ."

Joel placed one of his hands over hers. "Of course you didn't mean to split my head open. You were just passing the cookies, and the plate slipped out of your hand, right?"

"Oh, you! Cut it out!" She looked up at him, searching his face. His eyes looked dark in the gloom. "Can you. . .forgive me? I—I didn't mean to hurt you. . .I don't know what came over me."

He threw the towel on the pew and raised her hand to his lips. "Of course I forgive you. But do you forgive me for being an overbearing jerk? I guess I didn't realize you saw my actions that way. I just wanted to help. But if you need me to back off, I will. No more hounding you."

With those words, he kissed her hand.

It was at that moment, that second, when his lips touched her hand and his forgiveness touched her heart, that Val knew without a doubt how much she loved this man. How could she not love him? This beloved stranger who had barely left her side since she woke up in the hospital was a stranger no longer. Over the past seven months, she'd come to know his loyalty, his honor, his caring, his wacky sense of humor.

And now she realized that she loved him. She hadn't exactly "fallen" in love, rather, she'd "grown" into love with him. In one flash, she knew the truth. She *had* loved Joel before the accident. She'd loved him enough to marry him. And now she loved him again. She'd come full circle. That revelation filled her with a sense of completion. She caught her breath with its impact.

But it was too little, too late. Her heart sank. She'd made up her mind. It was too late to go back. There were some things that couldn't be changed.

Joel's lips lingered over her hand. His warm breath against her skin made her shudder, then blush, even in the dimness of the sanctuary. The moment seemed to stretch into infinity, until a heavy truck rumbled by outside, breaking the spell with a squeal of brakes.

Intently, Joel studied her face, then spoke. "Of course I forgive you, Val, but you know we can't go on like this."

She thought she heard regret in his voice. Maybe he'd come to the same decision?

"I know," she whispered, and sat with a thud as if she

were too weary to support the weight of her body any longer. She placed her hands on her knees and took a deep breath. "That's why. . .that's why I've decided to offer you your freedom, Joel."

"What?"

"Your freedom. I won't hold you to your vows."

"What are you saying?" The incredulity in his tone told her she might as well have said she was giving him the state of Idaho as a gift.

Gathering her courage, she summoned the speech she'd been rehearsing before he showed up with his bloody dish towel. Now that the moment had come, her heart was beating as wildly as a trapped deer's. She clasped her hands together to steady herself. "Isn't it obvious? I'm not the woman you married. I may never remember our marriage. I refuse to be guilty of pulling a bait-and-switch game on you. It's just not fair. You married one woman and ended up with another—"

"Yeah. . .so?"

"Don't interrupt! It's taking all my courage to get this out."

"Sorry. I'll keep my trap shut until you're finished." Joel sensed her turmoil and forced himself to keep silent.

Val hurried on before she lost her nerve. "Maybe even worse than not remembering you is that, well, I'm. . . defective." Even with the shadows cast by the stained-glass window slicing his face into planes, Val saw Joel's jaw tense. Her words tumbled over one another. "I've suffered a brain injury, memory loss, and personality changes. What if I can't hold a job? Or can't handle school? Or can never drive a car? What if I have more anxiety attacks, or have seizures again, like. . .Ruthie?"

Joel clasped the pew with both hands and leaned forward. "Let me see if I understand what you're telling me. You want to give me a divorce because, number one, you don't want to run a 'bait-and-switch' game—like a store offering certain merchandise but stocking something else at a higher price—and, number two, you're defective because your brain's been injured? Am I getting this right?"

Val nodded miserably.

His tone was low and deliberate. Even in the dusk, she could see his gaze, relentlessly penetrating. "Well, Val, I appreciate the guts it took to lay your cards on the table like this—not to mention your consideration of me—but I don't buy either line of reasoning."

Her defensiveness mushroomed. With a few words, he was dismissing all her hours of agonizing. Val swiped one hand down her face and began over. "Be reasonable, Joel. I can't sentence you to a life of misery. I don't know what our marriage was like before, but it had to be better than the bed of nails we walk on now. This isn't what you bargained for. Perhaps our marriage could be annulled since I'm not the same woman you married. Then you could start over with. . .with someone who could at least remember meeting you."

She had to choke out the last words.

"Finished?"

Val nodded.

"Well, I don't see any plates in sight, except maybe the collection plate, so I guess I'm safe," he quipped as he vaulted over the pew and sat beside her. "I've heard you out, now hear me out. Fair?"

"Fair." Her hands twisted in her lap.

"First, I appreciate your kind motives, but releasing

me from my vows exceeds your authority. That authority belongs to God and He says, 'What God hath joined together, let not man put asunder.' As for the 'bait-and-switch' analogy, it's just that. An analogy—that doesn't fit. Incidentally, in case you hadn't noticed, I'm not a bargain sweater or pair of boots. I promised to love you and stick by you in sickness and in the worst of times. In my mind, what's happened in the last seven months fits both those categories, wouldn't you agree?"

Val nodded silently, trying to swallow the lump forming in her throat.

"So, that leaves the 'defective' part," Joel continued. "We're all defective, Val. Original sin is the original defect. Our culture says that the only lives worth living are the useful and the perfect. I doubt if Dr. Death and his type would see much value in Ruthie's life, for instance. But that's not God's way. He loves each of us—not because of what we can do or how perfect we are. He loves us simply because we are His."

Val hardly noticed that he'd taken one of her hands and was gently chafing it between both of his, as if trying to warm her.

"I love you, Val, not because you can walk or run a marathon, or earn a master's degree in journalism. Sure, some things about you are different, but you're still my wife. Old Val, new Val—makes no difference. I love you. . .because you're mine."

Captured by his fervor, Val blinked back her tears. His words, and the love behind those words, were engulfing her like the summer sun flowing over a field of wheat.

"And as for defective," he said with a trace of amusement, "may I remind you that you married a defective? Yep, you married me, knowing full well that I'm a recovering alcoholic. Pretty defective, if you ask me. But you loved me enough to throw in your lot with me. Bottom line, Val, we're both defective, and we've both come short of the glory of God—along with the rest of creation. Who knows, maybe by this time next year, I'll have lost the use of my legs in an accident. I hope you'll be there to push my wheelchair. Every day." He paused, and Val knew he was choked with emotion. "I pray that you'll learn to love me again. . .because without your love, my life is a wasteland."

Val's heart swelled with love. Gratitude and wonder pulsed through her. Words formed in her throat, but she couldn't say them at first. Finally, haltingly, she released them. "But. . .I do love you, Joel."

His eyes narrowed. "You do?"

She nodded, blinking.

In one fluid motion, he drew her into his arms and sought her lips in a kiss that was long, searching, warm. She melted into his passion, feeling her own desire for him ignite in exquisite sweetness. When he pulled away and gazed into her face, his voice was low and pained. "I need you in my life, Val."

Her tears came, soft and cleansing. He gathered her against his chest and she leaned her head against his shoulder. He stroked her hair, whispering softly that he would always need her.

He needs you, princess.

Suddenly, Val's near-death vision of her parents floated back. "He needs you, princess," was what her father said about the faceless man in the cranberry sweater. Her purpose on earth wasn't finished yet because this man still needed her.

"It was you!" she cried, bolting upright, tearing herself

out of his embrace. "*You* were the one who needed me!"

"Hey, babe, that's me. The man who needs you."

She threw back her head and laughed, knowing Joel was staring at her in bemused puzzlement. Her love for him bubbled up inside like a cool mountain spring. That love gave her the peace, the security, the sense of belonging that she'd needed since she'd opened her eyes in the hospital and found herself facing a world of pain alone.

Yes, she needed him, too.

"I've got a story for you, Joel." Briefly, with great excitement, she related the experience, beginning with the tunnel of light, her angel, meeting her parents, experiencing Christ's forgiveness and healing, being told it wasn't her time to die. "My father said I had to go back because someone still needed me. I saw a man in a cranberry sweater running toward me, but I couldn't make out his features. . .then I fell backward through the tunnel and woke up to find my heart being jump-started."

"Cranberry sweater, huh? *I* have a cranberry sweater. A present from you, as a matter of fact. . ." Joel frowned, searching his memory bank. "Unless I'm mistaken, I was wearing that sweater the day of your accident. Yes. . .I was! I remember because afterwards, I put the sweater away. Didn't have the heart to wear it again. Too many bad memories."

Val watched the light from a passing car dance across her beloved's face. Her heart thrilled. It was true. She loved him and he loved her. She felt warm, safe, enthralled by the reality of their love. This was real! Their love had been tested in the furnace and had emerged bright shining gold. She didn't deserve such a precious gift, but her gracious God had given it to her all the same.

One nagging doubt remained. "Joel, my mood swings . . .the possibility of more panic attacks, or seizures—"

He squeezed her shoulders. "We'll handle them, together. Any problem is *our* problem. We'll take each one as it comes. You may never have another seizure, but if you do, it won't be the end of the world. I'll still love you and we'll cope."

She nodded, trying not to weep again. "But. . .but what if I never remember you from before?"

He put his hand to her face. "It's the present that counts, Val. We're together now, and that's all that matters. Sure, it would be nice if your memory returned, but if it doesn't, my feelings for you won't change." He paused for a moment, studying her eyes, then said slowly, "Do you know the purpose of Christian marriage? Why people get married? Mack shared this with me after you came out of the coma and didn't recognize me."

She put her head to one side. "What?"

"Well, this is how he put it, and it brought me comfort: Besides parenthood and the obvious love and companionship two people enjoy in a relationship, the great underlying function of Christian marriage is to help your mate become the person God created him or her to be."

Val caught her breath at the beauty of that thought. "Oh! It's the idea of destiny, isn't it? We're to help each other fulfill our destinies in Christ. How true! I never looked at Christian marriage quite like that before. But. . . how could that have possibly helped you when I couldn't remember who you were? We didn't have much of a marriage at that moment."

Joel ran his forefinger along her jawbone, an intimate,

possessive gesture. "It confirmed my faith that our marriage was in God's hands and that He was working His good plans for us. All the hard times—and I'm sure there will be more—are to help us grow in love in the Lord."

She let out a sigh of wonderment. "I can see how that helped keep your faith strong."

"We'll work hard on our marriage, Val. We'll go to Marriage Encounter, or see a counselor, or take couples' communication classes—whatever it takes to nurture our relationship and make it strong."

"Yes," said Val brightly. "Whatever it takes."

Suddenly, Joel remembered the inspiration that had struck him as he was dashing out of the house. "I have something for you," he said as he reached underneath his shirt and pulled out the pink envelope.

Val took the greeting card and read the neat printing on the envelope: "To my Val." The envelope had once been sealed, but now it was torn open. Puzzled, she drew out the card. An anniversary card. She smiled at the quaint lace and hearts. Her head shot up. "Did I miss something here? It's not our anniversary, is it?"

"No, it's not. Your memory is working OK. No, I gave you this card the night of your accident. I hid it in your purse. You must have opened it sometime before you got hit. Nurse O'Hanrahan at the hospital gave it to me with your stuff. Said you might want to have it again someday."

"Oh, Joel! I don't know what to say."

Suddenly all thumbs, she had to make two attempts to open the card. Inside, Joel had written:

Ten months today, lady. Ten months of love
and happiness. I'm not much good at poetry, but

*here goes: Roses are red, violets are blue, If I
had to do it over, Val, I'd still marry you. What
I'm trying to say, Val, is that I'd marry you all
over again.*

Joel

She looked at him, helplessly. How could she not give
him her heart completely? Placing the card in her lap, she
cradled his face between her hands, looking deeply into
his eyes. "And I would marry you again, Joel Bennigan."

His slow smile gained momentum, coming from the
deepest places of his heart. She knew she'd just made
him the happiest man alive, and that made her happy.
"Val, let's do that!"

"Do what?"

"Have another wedding. One you'll remember."

"Yes, yes, yes!"

"It'll celebrate the marriage of our hearts here and
now," said Joel, taking both her hands in his. "I take you,
Val, to be my lawfully wedded wife, to have and to hold,
in sickness and in health, in good times and bad, till
death parts us."

Val's response was measured and slow, heavy with
meaning. "And I take you, Joel, to be my lawfully wedded husband, to have and to hold, in sickness and in
heath, in good times and bad, till death parts us."

He kissed her, pressing his lips to her brow, her
cheeks, her chin, her mouth. When they pulled apart, he
whispered, "I've been waiting for you, Val. All my life."

She jumped to her feet and pulled him up. "Say, Mr.
Bennigan, do you think you could give a girl a ride
home? Seems as if I'm stranded here without trans-
portation."

He stood looking down at her and, even in the dimness, she could see his lips quirk in amusement. When he spoke, he affected a southern drawl. "It would be my pleasure, Mrs. Bennigan."

He stepped out of the pew and held out his hand to her. She took it and went to him. Then he pulled her close and they walked down the aisle. "But I was wondering, Mrs. Bennigan, if when we get home, you might care to come up to my room to see my etchings. . .eh, what I mean is, to watch my fish."

Val broke into laughter.

He hugged her waist, continuing his southern gentleman accent. "Not only that, but I happen to have a lady's wedding ring on my bureau that might just fit that pretty little finger of yours."

Val's heart was singing but she managed to put just the right amount of indignant shock into her voice. "Mr. Bennigan, are you suggesting what I think you're suggesting?"

"Why, Mrs. Bennigan, I assure you. . .my intentions are entirely honorable."

Suddenly her mood shifted. "Oh, Joel! Can we make it? Can we really start over again?"

"We'll make it—for better or worse." His sober expression matched her own. "We have a future because we have love—and love, remember, is of God and lasts forever."

"Forever," she whispered, savoring the sound of the word. Then she smiled and raised her hand to touch his face, feeling the healing warmth of his skin beneath her palm. "Love lasts forever. Of course. . .how could I forget?"

A Letter To Our Readers

Dear Reader:

In order that we might better contribute to your reading enjoyment, we would appreciate your taking a few minutes to respond to the following questions. When completed, please return to the following:

Rebecca Germany, Managing Editor
Heartsong Presents
P.O. Box 719
Uhrichsville, Ohio 44683

1. Did you enjoy reading *Tender Remembrance?*
   - ☐ Very much. I would like to see more books by this author!
   - ☐ Moderately
     I would have enjoyed it more if _____

   _____

2. Are you a member of **Heartsong Presents**? ☐ Yes ☐ No
   If no, where did you purchase this book? _____

   _____

3. What influenced your decision to purchase this book? (Check those that apply.)

☐ Cover	☐ Back cover copy
☐ Title	☐ Friends
☐ Publicity	☐ Other_____

4. How would you rate, on a scale from 1 (poor) to 5 (superior), the cover design? _____

5. On a scale from 1 (poor) to 10 (superior), please rate the following elements.

     ___ Heroine   ___ Plot

     ___ Hero   ___ Inspirational theme

     ___ Setting   ___ Secondary characters

6. What settings would you like to see covered in **Heartsong Presents** books? _____

_____

_____

7. What are some inspirational themes you would like to see treated in future books? _____

_____

_____

8. Would you be interested in reading other **Heartsong Presents** titles?   ❑ Yes   ❑ No

9. Please check your age range:
    ❑ Under 18   ❑ 18-24   ❑ 25-34
    ❑ 35-45   ❑ 46-55   ❑ Over 55

10. How many hours per week do you read? _____

Name _____

Occupation _____

Address _____

City _____ State _____ Zip _____

Only You

A Romantic Collection of Inspirational Novellas

Valentine's Day—a day of love, romance, and dreams. *Only You,* a collection of four all-new contemporary novellas from **Heartsong Presents** authors, will be available in January 1998. What better way to celebrate than with this collection written especially for Valentine's Day. Authors Sally Laity, Loree Lough, Debra White Smith, and Kathleen Yapp have practically become household names to legions of romance readers and this collection includes their photos and biographies.

(352 pages, Paperbound, 5" x 8")

Send to: Heartsong Presents Reader's Service
P.O. Box 719
Uhrichsville, Ohio 44683

Please send me _____ copies of *Only You.* I am enclosing **$4.97 each** (please add $1.00 to cover postage and handling per order. OH add 6.25% tax. NJ add 6% tax.). Send check or money order, no cash or C.O.D.s, please.

To place a credit card order, call 1-800-847-8270.

NAME _____

ADDRESS _____

CITY/STATE _____ ZIP _____

Heart♥ng

CONTEMPORARY ROMANCE IS CHEAPER BY THE DOZEN!

Any 12 Heartsong Presents titles for only $26.95 **

Buy any assortment of twelve Heartsong Presents titles and save 25% off of the already discounted price of $2.95 each!

** plus $1.00 shipping and handling per order and sales tax where applicable.

HEARTSONG PRESENTS *TITLES AVAILABLE NOW:*

(If ordering from this page, please remember to include it with the order form.)

······· Presents ·······

Great Inspirational Romance at a Great Price!

Heartsong Presents books are inspirational romances in contemporary and historical settings, designed to give you an enjoyable, spirit-lifting reading experience. You can choose wonderfully written titles from some of today's best authors like Veda Boyd Jones, Yvonne Lehman, Tracie Peterson, Nancy N. Rue, and many others.

When ordering quantities less than twelve, above titles are $2.95 each.
Not all titles may be available at time of order.

Heart♥ng Presents
Love Stories Are Rated G!

That's for godly, gratifying, and of course, great! If you love a thrilling love story, but don't appreciate the sordidness of some popular paperback romances, **Heartsong Presents** is for you. In fact, **Heartsong Presents** is the *only inspirational romance book club*, the only one featuring love stories where Christian faith is the primary ingredient in a marriage relationship.

Sign up today to receive your first set of four, never before published Christian romances. Send no money now; you will receive a bill with the first shipment. You may cancel at any time without obligation, and if you aren't completely satisfied with any selection, you may return the books for an immediate refund!

Imagine. . .four new romances every four weeks—two historical, two contemporary—with men and women like you who long to meet the one God has chosen as the love of their lives. . .all for the low price of $9.97 postpaid.

To join, simply complete the coupon below and mail to the address provided. **Heartsong Presents** romances are rated G for another reason: They'll arrive *Godspeed!*